T0355005

SANDRA B.

SANDRA B.

"It is all right to rat, but you can't re-rat."
– Winston Churchill

DONNA WARD

iUniverse®

SANDRA B.

iUniverse books may be ordered through booksellers or by contacting:

iUniverse
1663 Liberty Drive
Bloomington, IN 47403
www.iuniverse.com
844-349-9409

Because of the dynamic nature of the Internet, any web addresses or links contained in this book may have changed since publication and may no longer be valid. The views expressed in this work are solely those of the author and do not necessarily reflect the views of the publisher, and the publisher hereby disclaims any responsibility for them.

Any people depicted in stock imagery provided by Getty Images are models, and such images are being used for illustrative purposes only.
Certain stock imagery © Getty Images.

ISBN: 978-1-6632-6867-9 (sc)
ISBN: 978-1-6632-6868-6 (e)

Library of Congress Control Number: 2024923914

Print information available on the last page.

iUniverse rev. date: 11/13/2024

Something about this night was special. Crescent moon, winking stars, all pinned to an icy cobalt sky on New Year's Day, 1980.

"Happy New Year!" The Universe shouted to Ralphy P. as he stumbled home from his neighbor's party to let out Scraps the dog. The Brooklyn street was smooth and white with six inches of new snow, and Ralphy's foot missed the curb. He pitched face forward and let out a laugh at the Universe's joke, his *ha-ha's* piercing the calm in the tidy little neighborhood. He got to his knees and howled at the moon. "I'm alive!" he cried, and the night sky seemed to brighten at Ralphy's high spirits. He got stiffly to his feet and stumbled on, picking his way through the snow in search of the pathway to his house.

He'd built the path, brick by brick, in late August, and now he navigated its invisible L-shape by way of landmarks: *enter* at the two small cedars near the sidewalk, *turn right* at the statue of the Virgin on the lawn, *walk past* the bay window on the left, and *arrive* at the front door framed in Christmas lights. Scraps the dog whined desperately from inside while Ralphy's frozen fingers struggled with the lock. "Make it quick," said Ralphy, and the dog bounded outside, lifting a leg at the nearest shrub. He peed a long, continuous stream, blissfully unaware of his owner's presence, even when Ralphy kicked snow in his face to hurry him up. Scraps was unflappable.

But then there was a thump—maybe a clot of snow falling off the roof—and it raised the fur on Scrap's neck. He dropped his leg and ran back into the house, while Ralphy stared at the steamy yellow stain in the snow. "Some fuckin' watchdog," he muttered. He pulled the door shut, turned the knob to make sure it was locked, and followed his footprints back along the path. He was anxious to get back to the party. He was hungry, and they put all the good food out after midnight.

Ralphy paused to take a deep breath, and he watched his frosty exhaust— proof of his ongoing existence—with a relief so profound that it brought him to tears. For the past year he'd been on constant alert, eyeing every stranger, every slow moving vehicle, avoiding crowds and open spaces. Now, six months after the trial, six more wiseguys were in prison and Raphy P. was still standing. No one knew he'd worn a wire. No one ever suspected Ralphy P. of being a rat, and with sloppy, gin-martini gratitude, he made a New Year's Resolution to the moon and the stars. Ralphy P.'s informant days were over. He would never rat again.

"Happy New Year," said the Universe again, and Ralphy's eyes welled up as he raised his arms and waved to the heavens in a wordless declaration: *I made it! Ralphy P. is still alive!*

The crunch of snow behind him caught Ralphy's ear. Then another crunch, and he turned his head and blinked hard at a figure in a long dark overcoat moving toward him, galoshes cracking through the crust, picking up speed as the phantom bore down on him.

"Hey! Ralphy Pagano!" another voice called from the street, and Ralphy gaped stupidly at this second figure striding toward him with a jack-o-lantern grin on his face and a baseball bat tucked under his arm. "Hey, I got good news and bad news," said the jack-o-lantern, closing in. "The good news is you don't need to make a New Year's resolution. And this"—he swung at the air with the bat—"is the bad news."

They led Ralphy, one in front, one behind, on his last walk down the brick path. A gray sedan idled at the curb. Dumbfounded, and still mercifully drunk, he looked inside the open passenger door, then turned back to face his pursuers just as the bat came crashing down. One mighty crack crushed Ralphy's skull. It lolled off the side of his neck like a broken flower.

The men hoisted Ralphy's body like a bag of cement, and dumped it into the trunk. One of Ralphy's hands reached out, palm up, as if checking for rain. The bat-man slammed the lid on it, and when it failed to close, jabbed at the hand with his bat, stuffing it back inside. Moments later, when the body of Ralphy P. was fully contained and ready for disposal, they drove off into the New Year's Night.

Back at the house, Scraps howled mournfully for a while, then curled up on the rug and went to sleep. By two a.m., the neighborhood had settled back into wintry silence, and the universe carried on.

Five miles away, three men make their way home from Coney Island. They stumble and laugh as they pass around a bottle of Stolichnaya. With each gulp, a loud and raucus toast rings out in slurred, sloppy Russian.

They try to sober up as they approach their Brighton Beach neighborhood and their three modest houses, all in a row at the end of the street. It's quiet now, but for much of that day the muffled sounds of auto deconstruction had leaked onto the streets, from the house at the end, with the double-wide driveway.

They see the car parked in front and pass the bottle around again, toasting this promising start to the New Year. They look through the car windows, see the key in the ignition, and figure they'll get further instructions from the boss. That's how it works. One man unlocks the garage door and pulls it open, and another drives the car into the chop shop.

"It's clean," someone says, after scanning the interior and all the compartments for personal documents. "Check the back."

Someone opens the trunk. "Just a blanket," he says. Then, "Oh shit."

The other two join him, and stare into the dark space.

"Is that—"

"Yes."

"What do we do with it?"

"Leave it! We never saw it - *kapeesh?*"

One man pulls the heavy blanket over the gem encrusted Faberge Egg, tucking it in at the sides. Then, huddled together on this frosty night, they finish the bottle.

1

"Is there really *still* a Mafia?" Ken Schneider, supervisor of the New York FBI office, screwed up his eyes and repeated the question inches from the face of the rookie who'd asked it. "We're not tracking Santa Claus, Agent Tilly. We're not looking for extra-terrestrials in some East Podunk cornfield."

The glass-walled conference room was soundproof, but anyone looking in would see a trim, balding middle-aged man smacking a flip chart with his pointer and grinning maniacally at his subjects.

"What do these five names have in common, people?" He trained his eyes on Agent Tilly. "Any ideas?"

"They're all Italian?"

"Yes…and?" Schneider coaxed.

"They're the Big Five, with Sicilian roots. La Cosa Nostra, and we don't call them the Mafia." Tilly, on a roll, continued proudly, "And they've been mostly neutralized, through the efforts of this, and other FBI offices around the country— with some help from local law enforcement."

"And?" Schneider coaxed.

"Informants?"

"Exactly," replied Schneider, and scattered "ah's" came from the room, as if this was some sort of revelation.

Schneider did a grim, eyeball sweep of the assembled agents. "How many of you have attended at least one OC orientation?" There were ten men in the room. Four hands went up.

"Perfect," he said and rapped the floor with his pointer to show that it wasn't. "Anyway, the Five Families don't concern you." He flipped to

1

the next page. "These are your crime families, people. Benigno and Forte. Victor Benigno is into loan sharking, drugs, prostitution, rackets—the usual. Dante Forte is slightly less ambitious, mostly white collar securities fraud, art smuggling, and we think he might be a Benigno takeover target somewhere down the road. They are not the LCN Ivy League, but they're becoming more active. Until now they've been flying beneath our radar. Why do you think that is, Agent Tilly?" Schneider sat down, preparing for a long wait.

Tilly exchanged glances with his neighbors, none of whom had the answer. Then Tilly said, "What about the Russians?"

"The Odessa Mafia?" snapped Schneider, barely concealing his contempt for a totally irrelevant subject. "The Russians are not your problem." He jumped from his chair and rapped savagely on the floor with his pointer. "LCN 101, people! The answer to my actual *question*, Tilly, is *informants*! We don't have enough Benigno and Forte informants! Your first assignment," he barked, scanning the room, is to develop these sources, at least two of which will be T.E.I.'s –"

"Top Echelon," someone muttered.

"Well done, Agent Andrews. "And why are these sources referred to as Top Echelon?"

"Because they're highly placed within the Family."

"Correct," said Schneider, "High enough to have access to the Don."

"They still call themselves that?" Tilly whispered to his neighbor, "He's kidding, right?"

"Yes, the head of the Family is still referred to as the Don," Schneider explained wearily, adding, "And I never kid, Agent Tilly, I have no sense of humor, as my wife can tell you." Hands went up but Schneider ignored them. "Please direct LCN questions to your squad leaders—Agent D'Angelo for Benigno. Agent Oberlin for Forte."

Schneider looked out the window and watched a snow plow make its way north along 3rd Avenue. "Has anyone seen Agent Oberlin today?"

Mark Oberlin sat in the third car of a train to Greenwich, Connecticut. Sitting next to him was Sandra Benigno, wife of crime capo Victor Benigno. She was a bottle blonde, not a bad looking woman. Oberlin placed her in her late forties. Under the sable coat lurked a black knit mini dress, hiked to the hilt when she crossed her stiletto-heeled boots.

Oberlin was trained at being a good listener, a skill that came in handy today as he listened to Sandra talk, non-stop, from Grand Central Station to Greenwich, Connecticut, and then back again, to Grand Central. She provided murky details of a crime scheduled to take place the following Friday. And she demanded, as a taxpayer, that Agent Oberlin use every FBI resource at his disposal to stop it.

"You say you *overheard* all of this?" Oberlin reiterated, doubtfully. Mob wives were seldom involved in the Family business.

"Yeah. Either with my own ears, or mentally. I couldn't be sure. I'm a light sleeper, Agent Oberlin—"

"Please, just Mark." He glanced around to make sure they were alone. With the morning rush over, there was a well-spaced sprinkling of passengers in the car he'd selected, third from the end, making a quick escape possible in either direction, if needed.

"Okay, so I'm a light sleeper. Mark. Mostly because of the hours my husband keeps, what with his Family sit-downs and other bullshit excuses to get together with the boys, or with Miss Poland—" she noted his raised eyebrows—"his girlfriend! So Tuesday night I couldn't sleep and figured I'd make my sauce for Wednesday. There's a TV in the kitchen and while I was watching Carson I heard my husband talking about a job involving Russians with stolen cars and smuggled art and heart attacks... whatever that means. Maybe medical devices."

"Or maybe artifacts—"

"...and then someone else said he should use my son Billy as the front man. That's why I'm here, talking to you! Risking my own life to save my son!"

"I see," said Oberlin thoughtfully. "So...based on what you overheard with your own ears, or"—He made finger quotes—"*mentally*, you want us to intervene?"

"Of course! Isn't that what tax payers pay you to do!"

"Well, yes." Oberlin was pretty sure the Benigno's kept their tax bill very light.

"Look, it's my son I'm concerned about here!" she exclaimed loudly, as if talking to the hearing impaired. "Victor's always saying, *when's he gonna earn his keep?*" Her face congealed fluidly into slit-eyed fury. "I'll see Victor burn in hell before he puts my son in danger. You understand me? Mark?"

"Has Billy worked with his father before?" Oberlin replied mildly.

Now she grimaced, as if he had spinach between his teeth. "He's sixteen years old, for God's sake! You should know this stuff! The Feds have been following my family for the past five years! Where have *you* been?"

"Actually," said the thirty-one year-old Oberlin, "I became a Special Agent four years ago. I've been working white collar crime for the past two. Before that I worked out of the Michigan office—"

"Ugh, boring! I don't need your life story." She uncrossed her legs, pressed her back against the seat and released a deep, audible moan. Then she glanced around nervously, leaned in and whispered, "I guess I should mention that my husband is not Billy's father."

Oberlin raised a brow and leaned in through the curtain of *Givenchy Eau de Toilette.*

"I know. It's a shocker," she continued, "but there's more to it than that. Billy," she whispered, "is a Forte." She backed away for a better look at Oberlin's Irish schoolboy face, but it held the same credulous, open expression she had noticed the first time she'd met him, at a neighborhood Italian pastry shop, where she'd been standing at the counter, waiting to pick up her order. It was Oberlin's easy manner that had persuaded her to accept his offered business card and slip it into her pocket. *"You never know when you might need to talk to somebody you can trust,"* he had said.

"Have you ever seen Dante Forte?" Sandra said the name as if he were a Fellini movie star. "He's still gorgeous, but you should have seen him in high school. We all had a crush on him. We practically lined up in front of his house so we could walk to school with him. Well, not exactly *with* him, but a few blocks behind him, anyway. By the time we graduated, we'd all dated him—and I use the word *date* loosely, if you know what I mean."

"My turn came a little late, and the timing was not good. I was dating Victor—but don't judge me. Mark. Anyway, when I found out I was pregnant I told Victor it was *his* baby—to keep him from killing Dante. Bad enough he killed my brother, but that's another story." She followed his gaze out the window. "What. You've never seen snow before?" A moment passed. "Look, can you help me or not?" she said to the back of his head.

"I'm…processing."

"Well hurry up! We're almost back in the city."

Oberlin sat back and shrugged. "What, exactly, do you expect me to do?" He watched her, imagined the synapses firing away as she considered her options. How is it, he wondered, that a mob wife never considers the possibility that she might give birth to a future gangster.

"I want you to swear to me, Agent Oberlin, that you'll stop this thing from happening."

Oberlin found his service car, a light blue '78 Ford Galaxie, behind a snow drift on 3rd Avenue and 69th Street. He'd parked in front of a fire hydrant, his FBI plaque clearly visible on the dashboard.

Now the snow reached halfway up the door, swallowing the hydrant. After several attemps to unlock the door, he realized he'd be stuck in the city for the night, so he headed a few blocks west to his partner's apartment, and knocked.

"It's open."

Hayford Semple, fellow Quantico graduate—Class of '72—sat on a folding chair in the cramped space of his third floor walk-up. The only light came from a cheap table lamp, struggling to reach the corners of the small studio, and a moonbeam bouncing off the snow-covered fire escape. Against one wall, worn-out boxes were stacked almost to the ceiling. These were the earthly remains of his seven-year marriage.

"When do you plan to unpack?" Oberlin inquired, settling onto the other folding chair.

"Who gives a shit." Hay took a big swig of bourbon to show that he did not. "Does it bother you, Mr. Clean?"

"Not at all. Just thought there might be another lamp somewhere in that pile." He pulled out a recorder and placed it on the card table while Hayford poured out another bourbon. Then they listened to the flat, nasal voice of Sandra B., sporadically interrupted by Oberlin's deep monotone.

"Are you recording this conversation, Agent Oberlin? Or, should I?"

"I can't record you. Not without a court order." Several seconds passed. *"But there's no law against someone recording themselves, so if you'd like to do the honors...."*

"No, please, go ahead. I don't mind if you record me, just do it secretly."

"I can't do it secretly, now that you know I'm doing it."

"Look. Just don't record me saying that I know you're recording me! Okay?"

"Oh, Jee-sus," said Hay, with pain in his Carolina drawl. "Get to the dirty part!"

"I just turned forty-eight and I gotta say I'm in pretty good shape after two pregnancies and a twenty-five year marriage to the boss of a well respected Family. Just so you know, being married to a Family man didn't turn me into a hard, neurotic bitch with no outside interests. It's raising the kids and the whole domestic routine that did it –"

Semple made an *advance-the-tape* motion.

"—stolen cars, all BMW's, parked at a car dealership. All with new VINS, and dealer plates."

"Okay. So where does your son fit in?"

"I'm getting to that." A sigh. *"All of these cars..."*

"How many?"

"I think...I heard...three."

"Three cars?"

"*Yeah.*"

"*Hardly seems worth the risk.*"

"*It's not the cars Victor wants, it's what's inside one of them.*" A dramatic sigh. "*Stolen art, and I mean real, pricey art.*" A pause. "*Do you know what a Faberge egg is?*" She leaves a pause to let the wonderment of it all sink in, as if she just learned about Faberge eggs herself. "*They're parking the cars with fake dealer plates at a friendly dealership. The manager takes the payments for the Russians and gives the keys to the buyers. The Russians do it all the time. Only this time, there's this egg involved, and Victor wants that egg.*" After a pause, Sandra continues with a catch in her voice, "*I'm afraid for my son, Mark. Anything can happen as soon as money changes hands.*"

After several minutes, Oberlin clicked off the recorder. "So what do you think?"

"It's…Mark. I mean, have you really thought this through? That stuff about her son…"

"I know. You can't make this stuff up—"

"But *she* might have!" Semple shook his head wearily. "So you're prepared to request a full-scale criminal investigation based on the auditory hallucinations of a nut-job?"

After a thoughtful pause Oberlin said, "We need to get more resources for Benigno.

Semple downed a mouthful of bourbon and exhaled appreciatively. "Schneider's way ahead of you."

"What are you talking about?"

"We're reorganizing."

"Again? When did this happen?"

"This morning, while you were riding Metro North with a gun moll, Schneider created OC squads for Benigno and Forte."

"Where did he put me?"

"We're both on Forte."

Oberlin got up and noticed the caramel colored pool of melted snow at his feet. "Oh, sorry." He ducked into the kitchen and grabbed some paper towels. "Under the circumstances," he mused aloud while blotting up the slush, "I'll just ask for a transfer to Benigno."

"Better pass it by D'Angelo first. He's the Benigno squad leader."

"Who's the Forte squad leader?"

"You are."

"What?"

"That's right." Semple gave Oberlin's shoulder a hearty pat. "Congratulations, Mark. Looks like you're going places."

Oberlin sat down and picked up his glass. As the moonlight retreated from the fire escape, he processed his bourbon and pondered his Sandra B. conundrum in the dark.

As a career move, Oberlin's new OC assignment wasn't exactly a broad jump. The Forte Family, which had made its bones in the genteel world of art and securities fraud, had been ground zero for Oberlin's White Collar investigations for the past two years. These had culminated in a six-month trial for a pump and dump operation, sending Dante's top financial wizards to prison and threatening his white collar franchise with extinction. Oberlin's scrupulously developed pod of informants was still on the street, doing their own business as usual while Oberlin looked the other way. These criminals were untouchable—as long as they continued to rat out their Forte brethren—and this perverse, symbiotic relationship had sealed Oberlin's career trajectory, binding him to the Forte Family in the new OC squad formulation.

Oberlin's most valuable resource—a Top Echelon Informant known as Benny—was also his most difficult. A runty little guy, fiftyish, Benny managed to be in all the right places, all the time, and usually with an axe to grind. Benny ran the most expensive appliance repair shop on the lower East Side, which resulted in very few customers and plenty of time to concentrate on his core business— money laundering—which Oberlin ignored in exchange for Benny's *sine qua non* bugging skills. It would be no exaggeration to say that Benny was an idiot savant when it came to eavesdropping.

But as important as Benny's skills were to *We the People*, they were even more essential to the Forte crime family which, like its New York City competitors, was threatened with the breakdown of old-style omerta. Benny helped Dante Forte keep tabs on the Family through an ingenious intercom system which, had he filed a patent—and gone legit—would have made Benny a rich man. As always, with even the most loyal TEI's, Benny was a potentially dangerous Double Agent, should he ever gain the upper hand in this Agent-Informant relationship.

The loss of Dante's brokerage operation, as well as his smartest soldiers and wiseguys, had created a sizable dent in the Forte revenue stream, forcing Dante to rethink his career goals. He would need to adapt or risk being swallowed whole in a hostile takeover by Victor Benigno.

2

It was four-thirty on a gray, brittle January day. At the Benigno home a pot roast simmered on the stove, and the faint pulse of the grandfather clock ticked in the living room. Upstairs, Billy twisted a bobby pin into the lock of his sister's door. Clara was lying on her bed, princess phone in one hand, Mallomar in the other. A look of horror crossed her face as she watched Billy walk to her desk and rifle through her drawers.

"What are you doing?" she screeched. She threw the Mallomar at Billy's head and they both watched it hit the window with a loud splat.

"Fun's over, Clara. Where is it?"

"Where's what?"

"Stop fooling around. Where's my radio?"

"I don't know. Get out or I'll tell dad you're in my room without permission!"

"I'll tell mom you hid my stuff."

"You're such a jerk!" She hurled a pillow at him. "No one uses transistor radios anymore, you dork!"

He left, slamming the door hard enough to dislodge a painting of the Bay of Naples from the hallway wall. It cart wheeled down the stairs and hit the marble floor in the foyer with a sharp crack, the frame breaking in two.

"Shit."

"I'm telling," Clara screamed from the landing. She went back to her room and slammed her door, twice.

Billy gathered up the canvas and the broken frame and went into the kitchen to look for the wood glue. His mother was playing Canasta and wouldn't be home for another hour, giving him plenty of time to restore her favorite painting. But then he spotted his transistor radio next to the spice rack. He'd left it here three days ago with the power on, which meant the battery was now dead. In actual fact, even though it had started out as a radio, Billy had turned it into a one-way intercom with a small speaker and three-position toggle, one each for the hidden bugs in the kitchen, Clara's bedroom and his father's office.

He stuffed the device into his pocket, forgetting about the broken painting, and hopped down the flight of stairs between the kitchen and the entrance hall. The lower level of the Benigno house was a two thousand square foot rectangle with a series of special use rooms. Rec room with ping pong and pool table. Screening room with projection booth and feature film-sized movie screen. Weight room with a small running track. Lounge with a twenty-foot wet-bar. Three bedrooms. Three bathrooms. Sauna. This part of the basement was directly under the subfloor. To replicate natural light the builder had mounted backlit glass panels on the walls at twelve foot intervals, and these were framed by plastic hibiscus and other sun-craving species of fake flowering greenery.

There was a door where it looked as if the basement should end. It led to a room built beyond the footprint of the house on a cement slab. The door was made of reinforced steel and there was a keypad on the wall. Billy punched in a code, a combination of his and Clara's birthdates, waited for the click of the lock, and let himself in.

This secure underground facility was Benigno Central, where strategic planning, family mediation and made-man ceremonies took place, always late at night, never on the same day of the week.

An enormous round mahogany table surrounded by twelve high back leather chairs filled the room. At the far end, a recessed wood panel served as camouflage for another doorway. Billy pressed a spot at knee-height on the lower left side. The door sprang open and he walked a few feet into a dark tunnel, and stopped. The tunnel ran five hundred feet through the backyard, and connected to a former bomb shelter deep in the woods. Billy had walked that tunnel many times when he was a kid. One morning, when his mother thought he was on his way to school, he'd gone all the way to the end. He'd climbed up the ladder and tried to exit through the hatch cover, but the handle was too hard for his small hands to turn. He made his way back through the tunnel to the house, where he found the inside door closed and locked. He thought about banging on the door and yelling, but in the end—after an hour of struggling with the lock—he'd noticed the small metal shelf on the wall several feet above his head. It looked empty, but he instinctively reached for the closest extender he could find—a garden hoe—and scraped it across the shelf until the brass key fell to the ground. By the time Billy had staggered inside, heart racing and dripping with sweat, he'd decided to stay away from the tunnel forever. That was five years ago.

Back in the conference room, Billy ducked under the table and checked on his bug, a black plastic disc attached to the terminals of a 9-volt transistor battery. It was stuck with putty to the underside of the massive table, beyond the reach of light and the diamond pinky-ringed fingers of the soldiers who sat there.

He thought about Mr. Cataldo, how he'd probably freak out if he knew Billy had been able to wire the entire Benigno house just by watching him, Benny Cataldo, setting up an intercom system at the Forte family house. Dante Forte was his father's business competitor, but Victor let him go over there twice a week to help Lisa Forte with her math homework, maybe his way of sticking it to Mr. Forte because his son was smarter than Dante's daughter. Lisa was the hottest girl Billy had ever seen and he looked forward to her long blond herbal scented hair that fell around her shoulders and her cherry red lips that moved when she read a problem: *The sum of two consecutive integers is -9. What are the integers?*

Also in the freak-out camp was Billy's mother. Sandra nearly died from a heart attack—to hear her tell it—the first time Billy announced he was going over to the Forte house.

"What's wrong with helping a friend?" Billy had asked, as his mother bit down on her index finger.

"That friend? It had to be Lisa Dante?" And then Sandra had pretended to hyperventilate, which evolved into actual hyperventilation, forcing Billy to cancel the session with Lisa. Billy spoke to his putative father,

Victor, about this situation later that evening. "She's just protecting the family business," Victor told him, when in reality his wife was trying to protect her son's Dante-family jewels from his half-sister. Anyway, Victor liked the idea of having a family member in an enemy camp. He advised Billy to continue his visits to the Forte home, but not tell his mother.

3

Agent Tommy D'Angelo sat in a booth at the Regal Diner on Second Avenue, blowing into his bowl of steaming chili. Mark Oberlin slipped into the seat across from him. D'Angelo spooned himself a mouthful, then another, then said without looking up, "Schneider's looking for you."

"I know."

D'Angelo squared his muscular shoulders and sat back on the bench. "You missed an important meeting, Mark." His tone was friendly, but his large brown cow-eyes were expressionless, his smooth, thirty-eight year-old face undisturbed by emotion.

"I was approached by a Benigno source," said Oberlin, referring to Sandra B. "Thought you should know."

"Really?" D'Angelo feigned mild interest. "Who?"

"I can't tell you that, Tom."

"You're joking."

"They'll only talk to me."

"*They*? There's more than one?"

"I meant *he*."

"Okay. So who is *he*?" D'Angelo repeated in a reasonable tone.

"I told you."

"No. You told me you couldn't tell me."

"Right. And nothing's changed."

Without warning, D'Angelo smacked the table with his spoon, sending chili specks onto the head of an elderly man in the next booth. "That's my Family," he said through gritted teeth. "I'm head of the Squad! Didn't anyone tell you?"

"Sure. But apparently, no one told my source."

People stared at them, and the waitress looked concerned. D'Angelo sat back and pushed the bowl to the side, clearing the way for serious business. He leaned in and said softly, "So what's the deal?" When Oberlin hesitated he added, "C'mon, Mark. You can give me at least that."

"Auto and art smuggling."

D'Angelo chewed on this. "No way. My other T.E.s would have come to me with that."

"You would think. But the fact that they didn't—well, it could be significant." Oberlin cleared his throat. "I need corroboration, Tom. I need to talk to one of your people."

"Are you nuts!" Heads turned. He lowered his voice. "What a set of balls you have—"

"Look, I hate to have to state the obvious, Tom, but it sure looks as if you've been kept out of the loop."

"Yeah? And how do we know your source isn't full of shit, and just playing us?"

"We don't." Oberlin slipped out of the booth, leaving Tommy D'Angelo to consider his options.

Agent D'Angelo did a mental review of yesterday's daily briefing, which had been delivered in Schneider's typically acerbic style: *The decision has been made to implement a new strategic offensive. We know you've made real progress, and yes we've taken note of all the awards given out in this office for the solid case work that provided evidence for a record number of convictions. Therefore, we're going to try something different. Instead of just picking away at these fuckers, pruning their family trees, we're going to blast them out by the roots.*

The OC squads were expected to turn on a dime in a bureaucracy where it might take months for ideas to trickle down from the Sky Captains. This was the third Organized Crime initiative in the past eighteen months. Clearly something was not working out as planned. Clearly the LCN still had the upper hand, which is why the FBI—and not the Mob—was constantly shape-shifting. Not a good sign.

Nor, closer to home, did it bode well that Agent D'Angelo had not been informed of this latest Benigno Family initiative. D'Angelo dropped a ten dollar bill on the table, grabbed his coat and buttoned up on his way to the door. He needed to find the source of Oberlin's intel, and Carmine R.—D'Angelo's most reliable informant—would be his first stop.

Carmine Rizzo paced a path in the Jungle World exhibit at the Bronx Zoo. A large gibbon, baby clinging to her back, swung through the overhead trees and settled into the V of a limb to watch.

D'Angelo waited outside. He thought about surprising Carmine from behind, but then decided that the shock might be too much for his star informant. He waited for Carmine to double back in his direction, then caught his eye with a palms up—*what the fuck!?*

Carmine was a short, sporty, wiry little guy, around fifty. He glanced to his right, his left and then over his shoulder before saying with a nervous laugh, "What's goin' on?"

"You're supposed to tell me, Carmine. That's how it works."

"Tell you what? You're kidding, right? Unless—did I miss something?"

"Cut the crap, Carmine. Tell me a story."

Carmine pulled a pack of unfiltered Chesterfields from his yellow all-weather fisherman's jacket. "You got a light?" he said, and when D'Angelo made no effort to check, he patted himself down until he found a pack of matches. He lit up and took a long drag, holding it in like a lungful of weed, then letting it drift out through his clenched jaw. Carmine was in a deep funk, and sinking fast. "I don't like this," he croaked, shifting his weight from one foot to the other, bobbing back and forth, like a small Hudson River buoy. "I can't be seen with you."

"Right. So let's do this quick." D'Angelo's voice was hard, but Rizzo had such a baleful look on his face that D'Angelo relaxed his shoulders, and flashed a tight smile. "Okay, so you forgot to tell me."

Rizzo shook his head. "I got nothin', Tommy. I swear." His eyes were round with fear. "*You* wanted to see *me*, remember?"

"So you bring me all the way up to the fucking zoo?"

"I couldn't take a chance on being seen with you, Tommy. They'd never come here."

"Why not? We're surrounded by gorillas. All you goombahs should feel right at home." D'Angelo let out a grunt of disgust and took a step back. "I'm cutting you loose, Carmine."

Carmine caught D'Angelo's coat sleeve and lunged into his space, locking eyes inches from his face.

"You can't do this, Tommy."

D'Angelo yanked his arm away and calmly smoothed his sleeve. "There's nothing to worry about, Carmine." He looked at the ground now, because he was lying.

"Tell me straight-up, Tommy. Why are we here? You heard something, right?" Rizzo's voice was high, squeaky. "Hey," he said, with pleading eyes, "We had a deal. Whatever happens, you're supposed to look after me! That was the arrangement!"

"Yeah, yeah," D'Angelo said quickly, thinking *yeah, sure.* His top informant was now a compromised source, and as such, completely useless.

"Tommy, you gotta tell me what's goin' on. You gotta hide me somewhere, okay?" Rizzo glanced around quickly, then retracted his head into the collar of his coat, like a turtle. "You know them. They don't waste any time."

D'Angelo certainly did know this. In fact, D'Angelo fully expected his informant to be picked off as soon as they left the zoo, which is why he decided to take a detour and put some distance between them on the way out. At the 183rd Street entrance on Southern Boulevard D'Angelo hailed a cab and took off in a cloud of dust. He couldn't hear Carmine with the windows rolled up, but by his posture—arms in the air like he was holding up the world—he must have been saying, "Tommy! You fucking snake!"

D'Angelo sat back in the seat. All informants get a little hinky when they see an associate get picked off, and news of Ralphy P. would have leached into the underworld minutes after the positive ID of his various remains. D'Angelo didn't give a shit about Carmine, or about any shithead wiseguy who tries to buy back his life, however he did have a professional duty to prevent sources—*the most effective weapons in the OC arsenal*—from drying up. D'Angelo would stand by Carmine Rizzo, though not too close. And first thing in the morning he would spell out Carmine's options for him, provided the little rat managed to survive the night.

The first thing Carmine realized, after what a prick D'Angelo turned out to be, was that he, Carmine, made a perfect target standing on the corner of Southern Boulevard in his dayglo yellow jacket, his big deal Christmas present from the wife. Right away a cab pulled up. He hopped back onto the sidewalk to show he wasn't interested. As soon as that cabbie drove away, another pulled over. Carmine kept walking, not looking at anything but the ground, keeping his head low and his hands in his pockets, the right one wrapped around his Beretta.

"But look how roomy the pockets are, Carmy. I know you like that," the wife had said when he told her to take the ugly piece of shit back to the store.

Why the hell am I thinking about this now?

He started walking south to 187th Street, figured he'd turn at the corner and walk to Arthur Avenue. Carmine didn't like all the cabbies stopping, like they'd been sent to pick him up. Arthur Avenue was his territory. He knew every face, every car, and the cabs didn't just stop for no reason. Of course, everyone, meaning every wiseguy, knew Carmine's face too. And they knew all the lead agents working O.C., including Tommy D'Angelo. Even if Victor Benigno had no reason to suspect he'd been working for D'Angelo, it sure as hell would look that way if someone had seen them together. Dayglo yellow coat or not, Carmine was a sitting duck.

He whistled softly... *whenever I feel afraid I hold my head up high*... and walked casually for several minutes before reaching the corner. He turned and walked down the one-way street, his back to oncoming traffic. But there was no traffic here. It was quiet, away from the avenue, eerily empty for a big city street. He noticed his own rhythmic pace as his boots crunched into the snow. He heard a winter bird twitter, in a sweet song that died at the sound of tires skidding and a car turning onto his street. Carmine felt the hair on his neck jump to attention. He turned his head slightly and glanced over his shoulder at the slow moving black sedan.

On a normal Tuesday afternoon in Carmine's life, an approaching black sedan would be a normal occurrence. But today wasn't normal. Nothing about it was normal, from the minute Carmine got out of bed, and the wife said we need to talk, to three hours later when Tommy D'Angelo showed up at the bakery and said they needed to talk.

"But not here!" Carmine had pleaded, and Tommy had agreed to their rendezvous at the zoo. Now, Carmine felt with the certainty of the doomed that Victor Benigno's men had seen Tommy D'Angelo at the bakery. This, in and of itself, was not unusual. The G-Men knew all the best Italian eateries and bakeries, and they were treated cordially by the Family owners. But something had changed, someone had ratted him out, and Victor had put a tail on Carmine as soon as he left the shop to meet with D'Angelo.

He was sure of this narrative. He was sure he would die today, and he felt his blood still pumping away, but already turning cold.

But then, like a saintly aura, calm descended on Carmine. His brain told him to run, but his legs moved slowly as he walked down the street, taking note of alleyways, backyards and fences, all possible means of escape. And he noticed the people. Kids in strollers, the delivery man in front of a door a few houses up.

Some teenagers were walking towards him, laughing and joking. He kept his eyes on them, noticed how they spread out as they got closer, maybe wanting to force the old guy in the ridiculous jacket—*Hey, watch it, Dayglo Man!*—off the sidewalk and into the dog shit at the curb. While he was thinking this the black sedan pulled up behind him. He heard the gear shift into park, and the low idle of the engine. A car door opened, but did not close.

The kids were almost in Camine's face, swaggering and laughing. He gripped his gun, eased it out of his pocket. But then the kids stopped laughing, stopped moving. They stared past Camine. In one movement, they all took a step backward, then dove behind a parked car.

19

Carmine watched his gun hand rise, as if it belonged to someone else.

"Don't be stupid Carmine." The voice behind him was friendly. "Drop to your knees, slowly." But Carmine was frozen in place. It wasn't him standing there. It was him watching himself. "Do it now Carmine." He felt himself go down like a curtsey, arms held out to the sides. "Drop the gun, Carmine." It dangled off his fingers then fell to the sidewalk. It didn't go off when it hit the ground. Not like in the movies. But just the clank of metal on concrete made the kids take off down the street.

He crouched low and made a ball out of himself and pictured Ralphy P.'s head stuck on a fence at the landfill. They'd torn off his lips with pliers and shoved them through his ears with a screwdriver, right into his brain.

Two, maybe three of them came up beside him. They pulled his arms behind his back and cuffed him, then pulled a hood over his head and hauled him to his feet. The guy who patted him down said, "Oh, Christ."

Carmine knew he must have pissed himself.

They pushed him down to the floor in the back of the car, his head on the hump and his knees pressed against his chest. *As long as the car is moving I will be alive,* Carmine thought, and he hoped for a long trip. On the edge of panic he considered his situation, wondered whether he had any bargaining power with the Family, or maybe could cut a deal with these guys. *Who were these guys,* he wondered. The car was dirty and smelled like crap. No self-respecting wise-guy would drive around in a heap like this, so Carmine figured it must be just some punks trying to come up in the ranks with a fresh kill. He was both insulted by this lack of regard, and scared shitless that these *gavones* would miss and leave him a drooling vegetable. Carmine said a silent prayer to Mother Mary that they were packing enough fire power to kill him quickly, not some girly-shit pistol like a pearl handled baretta. Some of the wise guys used these as their *dress guns.* On a recent mob hit someone pumped five of these bullets into Enzo (Endzone) Rispoli's head, point blank, and Endzone just stood there, swatting at his head where the bullets hit like he was chasing mosquitoes. "Why the fuck did you do that?" he kept asking the shooter, who was Enzo's friend. The shooter was so creeped out that he bolted, and Enzo survived until the next day when a bigger gun was sent to finish the job.

They traveled for twenty minutes, maybe more, then suddenly slowed to a crawl. The driver said, "I need a buck fifty," and a few seconds later, "No, this is an exact change lane."

"Get into another lane," said the guy in the back seat.

"Why? Don't you have six quarters."

"No."

"A bill and two quarters?"

"No! I told you I don't have it. Move to the right lane." Then, "I said right, not left."

They were coming to a manned toll booth. A heavy plastic sheet was draped over Carmine's back and head. The guy who couldn't find exact change propped his feet on Carmine's back. There was no chance the toll taker would notice him.

Carmine was certain they were now on the Thruway heading upstate, that he was being taken to a cabin in the woods, one with a wood chipper out back. This is what he thought about for the next thirty minutes. When they reached their destination they pulled him from the car, pushed him through a door and sat him in a chair.

"I'm taking the hood off," said the driver's voice. "The cuffs stay on."

Like I got a choice, the thought. And then he was staring into the dull fish-eyes of his killer.

"Hello, Carmine," said the killer in a friendly tone. "I'm Special Agent Mark Oberlin. Agent D'Angelo said you might need some assistance."

So Carmine, in his panic, had misjudged D'Angelo, slightly. D'Angelo had alerted two other agents—Oberlin and Semple—who had picked him up, brought him to this motel, and made him comfortable. When Agent Semple left, Oberlin asked Carmine if he was hungry or thirsty, or if he needed to use the john. *He's either a real nice guy or full of shit,* thought Carmine, but he knew he'd find out which one soon enough.

Oberlin sat on the edge of the bed, opened up a Lipton tea bag and dunked it, in and out, in and out, into a Styrofoam cup, telling Carmine that he had a very good proposition for him if he answered a few questions.

"Like I got a choice?" Camine said. But he had a few questions of his own before he would tell this FBI agent squat. "Why didn't you guys identify yourselves on the ride up here?"

"Didn't we? Well, that's not right. You must have been very apprehensive. Please accept our apologies."

There it was. The bullshit.

"And should we expect your thanks, Carmine, for probably saving your life?" Oberlin offered his signature smile, the earnest Irish boy who went to church *and* took communion every Sunday.

"Okay, forget I even mentioned it." Carmine shook his head, as if to clear it. "I was just freakin' out on the floor of that car – which, I might add, is filthy."

"I'll inform the Bureau's garage of your observation."

Carmine smiled. This dorky guy would probably do just that. "So what's the deal you have for me."

"I need some information about the Benigno's."

"Look, I already told D'Angelo. I got nothing. Don't you guys compare notes?"

"Not really. No."

"Even if I did have something, what's in it for me? Why should I cooperate? Even if I'm not a dead man yet, I'll end up dead later if I work for you."

"We all end up dead later, Carmine. In the meantime, why not switch families? I'm sure Dante would welcome an ex-Benigno to the table, especially someone with pyrotechnic training."

"Pyro – oh, yeah, explosives." He'd done his research, Agent Oberlin. Camine had worked for the Luzzi Fireworks Family twenty years ago, after a stint on the bomb squad during the war. It was a miracle he was still in one piece, and he intended to keep it that way. "Victor's gonna ask me why this sudden interest in switching Families. Benigno has to give his blessing."

"Is that how it works?"

Oberlin acted like a Fed right off the cabbage truck, but Carmine knew better, figured he was just stroking him now, but he decided to play along. "Yeah. It's a sign of respect between families. The whole thing is like a job interview at a big company, Agent Oberlin. There's an interview, a background check and I need references from my previous employer, in this case Victor Benigno, who might already have put a hit out on me."

"*Might*, Carmine, is the key word." Oberlin beamed a wide toothy smile, finished his tea, and sat back in his chair, telescoping to Carmine he was getting down to business. "Look, Carmine, I understand that you're concerned about your physical well-being, and rightly so, but there's no avoiding the fact that you've got to roll the dice. Now, If you feel sure your cover's been blown, I can help you disappear as long as you understand that there's no turning back."

"And the other option?" Carmine knew what it was, but he wanted to hear Oberlin say it.

"We're back to the vagaries of the word *might,* I'm afraid."

"In English, Oberlin."

"In the best case scenario, the Family has no idea that you've been working for us. Go through the process, appeal to Dante on the basis of your value-added."

"What value added?"

"Your talent for exploding things, for one. But Dante knows that your bakery caters to a very upscale clientele, who would be a good source of revenue for any of his new brokerage scams. So go for it, Carmine, and don't look back. In my professional opinion, if your cover had been blown, we wouldn't be talking right now."

Carmine thought about this, figured he had no real choice. What was he supposed to do, abandon the eight-room house he'd just finished paying for and tell his wife and mother-in-law they were going underground? They'd rat him out themselves.

As far as working for Dante, he really had to admit it wasn't such a bad idea. Benigno and Dante hated each other's guts, and were always fighting for a bigger piece of the pie. The Dante Family might even offer him better protection. He said to Oberlin, "Okay, but if I go, I go legit. My informant days are over."

"Understood."

Carmine narrowed his eyes. Oberlin was reasonable, the kind of Fed that'll suck you in if you're not careful. "So tell me something. What's in it for you?"

"Just tell me what you know about the Benigno family."

"What, like family with a big F?"

"No, the Benignos themselves."

"There's Victor, Alessandra, Clara and Billy. Victor is your typical macho, mama's boy combo. Made a real big deal about being loyal to his wife and a good father to the kids. Clara's around twelve, and the apple of his eye, but you could see some changes coming, getting moody and mouthy if you know what I mean. He has a lot of patience, for the boss of a large criminal organization. She can do no wrong as far as he's concerned."

"It's a different story with Billy. He just turned sixteen, and he's a big mouth like all the other kids his age. He and the old man go at each other all the time. Mostly they fight over the kid wanting to be in the business, and the old man trying to keep him out of it. Once I heard the old man say to him, 'You want a place in the business? I'll give you a place. I'll put you where you'll take a bullet to the head.' Pretty strong words from a father, right? But the kid can be a real little dick. Who could blame a father for blowing his top every now and then."

"Tell me more about Victor," prompted Oberlin.

"Victor is a dangerous man. In my ten year association with the Family I know of at least fourteen hits he ordered. But putting a hit out on someone is a lot easier than beating them to a pulp with a baseball bat, or even shooting a guy in the head, so I can't really say if he was physically tough. I figured he was all bark when it came to Billy because no Family man would ever hurt his own son."

4

Victor Benigno nurses a double espresso at a cozy bistro table at Palermo Gardens. His consigliere listens to his State of the Family address, but keeps his mouth shut.

"So things are good, business-wise, according to the financials. Revenue up 60% over last year, due to our entry into the art world. As for losses, they began a downward trend as soon as I put a few disloyal associates out of commission. It's not something I like to do, but sometimes I have no choice but to remove impediments to the business. Take Ralphy P. He made a squeal deal with the Feds to save his own sorry ass from going to the slammer. None of my men suspected he was wired. Dumb shit probably figured he was home free. But business is business and rules are rules."

"Yeah, business is good, and maybe about to get even better. Dante's on the balls of his ass, the Feds being all over him these days. Typical FBI MO. One big bank robbery or embezzlement case hits the news, and before you know it every G-Man is assigned to White Collar, as if lightning will strike twice in the same place. Of course, that leaves fewer agents to cover the docks, which suits me just fine."

"So, Dante doesn't know it yet, but he's about to be acquired. I hope the takeover will be friendly, in fact I'm prepared to make the Forte Family a very nice offer in addition to giving Dante the co-chairman seat. I didn't see how he can refuse. Without fraud, embezzlement, insider trading and forgery, there's no other way for him to make a living, and he knows it."

"Some of his men are very talented, especially the guy who rigged his wiretaps. I need someone like that to keep tabs on the Family, to keep everyone honest, maybe avoid another Ralphy P."

Victor Benigno motions for a refill of the tiny cup. He waits for the waitress to walk away, and continues.

"Yeah, business is good. I could be very happy if I had stayed single. I don't love my wife, but I'm used to her being around, and every time it crosses my mind that I could get rid of her very easily, I think of the little ways she is not a pain in the ass. Know what I mean? She never interferes with my love life, she takes great care of the kids. Sandra wasn't exactly a beauty, but she was the only unspoiled merchandise in a very tough neighborhood. She isn't exactly easy going, either. No sense of humor. Worries about everything."

"If you ask me how we ended up together I'd have to say someone put a gun to my head, because it was true. I got her banged up and her brother came to my door with a semi-automatic under his coat. I invited him in but he just stood in the doorway, pointing the gun, and asked if I was going to marry his sister. At the exact moment I said yes, one of my men blasted away the back of his head, so I'm not sure he ever heard me. But I'm a man of honor. I keep my word. So I married her and we had about ten good years together, until Billy grew a mouth. My big problem with Billy is that he wants to be in the business. It's dangerous, I tell him, but how do you stop a sixteen year-old?"

5

Mark Oberlin sat on a sleek leather sofa reading a paperback and waiting for Benny Cataldo. He glanced at his watch and would have waited five minutes more, but the Bloomingdales sales associate asked him to go sit somewhere else. "You're making a dent in the leather," he said to Oberlin.

Oberlin intercepted Benny at the entrance to Home Furnishings. They rode the UP escalator to the Housewares floor, where they reconvened in front of Small Appliances.

Oberlin said, "I need your help, Benny."

Benny examined the specifications on the back of a Microwave Oven. "The first Microwave was the size of a refrigerator. Did you know that?"

Oberlin rolled his eyes. "I'm running out of time here."

"Okay, okay." Benny smiled slightly, an enigmatic pursing of the lips whenever he felt a deal, or a lie, coming on. "I'll help. But nothing too strenuous, okay?"

"It's Victor." Oberlin said sotto voce, even though they were alone.

"Victor?" Benny repeated in a whisper, avoiding Oberlin's eyes. "What's he got to do with me?"

"I heard something about a job at a car dealership, next Friday."

"Not my business, Mark. Not yours either. Doesn't tight-ass D'Angelo work that beat."

Oberlin sighed, not in the mood for more explanation, particularly since he had none. "I know the Family meetings take place somewhere on or near the Benigno house in Scarsdale. D'Angelo's never been able to pin down the location."

"What about his inside guy?"

27

Oberlin shook his head. "Says he doesn't know."

"What do you want me to do, Mark? I have a feeling you're gonna ask the impossible."

"Can you sweep the house for bugs?"

"How the hell can I get into the Benigno house?"

"It can be arranged."

Benny C. narrowed his deep set brown eyes. "My nephew from Palermo married a New York girl to get a green card. He just got a letter from the INS. They're conducting a fraud interview. I want you to make sure he passes."

Oberlin whistled. "That's a different agency, Benny. I can't—"

"Use your connections." Benny smiled. "That's what I want."

Oberlin straightened up, looked out at the mostly empty sales floor, then gave Benny a serious look. "How long will it take to find the bug?"

Benny shook his head. "Do we have an agreement?"

"Yes. I thought it was implicit," said Oberlin.

"Maybe I'm a little slow," said Benny. "Don't you need my nephew's number?" He held out a wad of paper. Oberlin took it and slipped it into his jacket pocket. "How many levels in the house?"

"Three."

"I'll need an hour. I'll do the lower level first, check the seams for conduit wire—"

"Whoa, Benny! No details, please."

"What. Not interesting enough for a G-Man?"

"No. I think what you do is fascinating, really. But if I have to take the stand in this case, which I'm sure will happen, it will be very helpful if I can swear under oath that I am not technically inclined—should the question arise as to where I got my information."

"Oh, I get it. What you're asking me to do is a federal offense and you don't want any part of it."

"Not exactly. I want the only part that matters to me. Confirmation that the house is bugged."

"Sure, Mark," he said, touching the side of his nose. "You know, you're no different from me or anyone else. We all want what we want."

"The difference," said Oberlin, "is that what I want is for the greater

28

good." He looked at his watch, realized he was late for his next appointment and walked quickly across the floor towards the elevator bank.

He stepped into a waiting car and rode down to Ladies Shoes on Five.

It always amazed him, women's love of shoes. There was almost no one in the housewares department, but here, amidst designer pumps and thigh high fur boots, pods of women were spending time, and considerable money, on fashion for the foot.

There were no men, except for Mark Oberlin and the young sales clerk who greeted him.

"Can I help you, sir?"

Oberlin gave the young man a stiff little salute. "My wife is interested in stiletto heeled black silk pumps."

"Okay." The young man looked over and around Oberlin. 'Where is she?"

"At the hospital," said Oberlin absently, watching an attractive blonde push several shoe boxes away with her red-lacquered toe. "Excuse me." He went over and sat in the chair beside her. "Hello Sandra."

She peered at him with eyes that Oberlin noted were green. "Who the hell are you?"

"Agent Oberlin?"

She peered at his full beard and mustache. "Oh my God!" She cackled. "What's with the facial hair?"

"Shh." He scanned the area, then said, "It's my disguise. Can we talk here?"

"This was your idea, Agent Oberlin."

"Please, Mark."

"Yeah, Mark, whatever. You're the expert, so why ask me if we can talk here?"

Oberlin smiled broadly, as if she had just told a really funny joke. "Can you keep your voice down just a little?"

"No problem," she replied loudly.

29

"Right. Okay, I've set up the sweep. My guy needs two hours."

Sandra B. reached into her Louis Vuitton handbag and pulled out a set of keys. "Make sure he's out in two hours." She watched Oberlin nod his head encouragingly. "I'm risking my life for my son, Mark. Just keep in mind I'm a dead woman if anything goes wrong."

One row over, in a chair facing the mirrored wall, a teenage girl watched them. She put her shoes back on, grabbed her two shopping bags and hurried off. She wondered who the guy with the fake beard was, and why Billy's mom had given him her keys.

6

The FBI conference room was crowded and hot, the aroma of coffee and shaving cream added to the funky scent of testosterone from the rookie male agents, and a trace of despair from management.

"It's all about informants, people. They are the keys to your success. I cannot stress too often or too strongly that your investigations are only as airtight as the sources you use. These sources must remain strictly confidential, for your ears only. And your informant relationships must be inviolable."

Ken Schneider's daily briefing was getting briefer by the day. He was worn out, and out of answers when his agents were still full of questions. He looked at the sea of faces, some seasoned pros but most were rookie agents new to the vicious world of Organized Crime. Here was one of them now, standing outside his open door, and Schneider pretended to be too busy to notice. He sat hunched over his desk, staring at piles of documents, then reached for his coffee mug on the far left corner, and made a wide arc around the edges of the desk before bringing it to his mouth, thereby protecting the paperwork from the coffee that reliably spilled, instead, onto the carpet.

"Ken, can I have a word?"

He said, "I'm all ears, Oberlin," without looking up. Oberlin noticed then that he had large, cabbage shaped ears. He started to close the door but Schneider barked, "Leave it. It's stuffy in here."

"This is confidential, Ken."

"This is an FBI office, Oberlin. The whole damn place is confidential."

31

With a grunt of annoyance he got up and pulled the door closed with a bang. "How's that?"

"Fine, thanks."

"You're sure? No Cone of Silence?"

Oberlin laughed politely, then coughed and said, "I'd like to transfer to Benigno, if it's not too much trouble."

"Can't do it," Schneider said flatly, explaining—with the caveat that he owed no explanation—that he had formed the squads according to logical resources. "Why do you want Benigno? You, a rookie, were selected for the Forte squad— Captain of the Team—because of your stellar performance in White Collar. And if your reports are accurate, all your sources are on the Forte side."

"I might have access to a Benigno informant," Oberlin replied evenly.

"Well then, I guess you'll have to introduce the gentleman to someone on the Benigno squad. See how easy it is?" Schneider got up heavily, and opened the door, giving Oberlin no opportunity to voice his reasonable concern:

How will I be able to keep my Benigno source absolutely confidential and my relationship inviolable if I am working on the Forte O.C. squad?

7

Dante Forte sat in the back of Little Venice Trattoria on Arthur Avenue, contemplating a large bowl of vongole that he didn't really want. He glanced out the window where two of his men were stationed near the door. He checked his Rolex, then looked down into his bowl and complained to the mussels, who clearly had problems of their own. "Mr. Carmine Rizzo has a meeting with Dante Forte, and he doesn't have the sense of propriety to show up a little early."

Things were not going well for Dante. Everything he touched these days seemed to be cursed. The authorities were moving in on him from all sides, and too many of his top men were in prison. He knew it was just a matter of time before they got bored and decided to cooperate with the government. Even though he'd been careful, over the years, to keep a legal arms length distance from the actions of his associates, the government was coming up with new strategies, on a daily basis it seemed, to fully implicate Dante Forte in the ongoing criminal investigations into his past business practices.

Who, he asked himself, was providing information to the FBI? Could there be rats in Forte Holdings LTD? The answer was yes, there could be, because no business is immune from infestation. He had no doubt that he would find the weak link, and take care of the matter in a civilized, low profile manner, not being one to condone the mutilation of bodies as a warning to potential transgressors. Not being particularly religious or superstitious OR particularly vindictive, Gentleman Dante Forte believed that the mere threat of death, and not the manner, would do the trick.

Before embarking on an intensive effort to secure the family business, Dante would wait to see what Victor Benigno wanted to discuss at their conference Friday night. As for Carmine Rizzo, the bakery shop owner who worked for Victor Benigno, he apparently had an interesting proposition for Dante. Their meeting had been arranged by Benny C. who had discovered through his own sources that Carmine was unhappy with the Benigno family and was seeking a change. Wearing the hat of Mob Headhunter, Benny claimed to have fully vetted Carmine, found him to be reliable and, more importantly, in possession of a unique skill that Dante would be needing.

As required by formal inter-family guidelines, Dante had contacted Victor Benigno as soon as he had received word of Carmine's interest. Any defections needed very close scrutiny for the good of both Families. This would not be the first time a rat looked for another clawhold while the ship he was on was sinking—especially if he was the one who had gnawed a hole in the hull.

If Victor was surprised at this personnel shuffle, he never let on. In fact the conversation between the two bosses could not have been more amiable. Benigno had said, "So be it." He hadn't even requested a replacement from Dante's own stable.

"So what's wrong with the guy?" Dante had asked Benny. "Why is Benigno making this so easy?"

"What I figure, Mr. Benigno, is that Carmine wants too much. He's getting too expensive for what you call his value added, which is making explosives. But don't worry about his standing with the Feds. According to my sources, he's still flying under their radar."

Of course, this brought up the question of who Benny's Fed sources were, and how cozy he was getting with them. You couldn't trust anyone anymore and the whole thing gave Dante Forte a huge migraine. He would have gone home to his den to listen to Puccini, but at that moment Carmine R. was escorted to his table. "Thanks for taking the time to see me, Mr. Forte," said Carmine.

Dante Forte nodded toward the chair across from him and Carmine sat down heavily, his yellow storm coat making crunching sounds on the seat. Dante pursed his lips and took in the sight of Carmine R. He hadn't expected a renaissance man, but Carmine was barely washed, and he was missing the tips of the index and middle fingers of his left hand. "Hazards of the trade, I guess," said Dante.

"What—oh, this?" Carmine held up his gnarled hand and looked at it with amusement. "No. These two digits came off me on prom night. Chick slammed a car door on them." More crunching as Carmine leaned across the table and said in a low voice, "Never had an explosives accident, Mr. Forte. Never will, either," he added, poking the table with his finger stubs for emphasis.

Carmine waited respectfully for Dante Forte to leave the table—and the tab—then put down cash and made his way to the door. He watched Dante and his two aides-de-camp get into a black town car and drive off. Carmine crossed the street to his own car, which was partly hidden by a trash bin. He got in, drove around the corner and pulled up alongside a phone booth.

"It's done. I'm in."

"Good," said Mark Oberlin. "It looks like your worries are over, Carmine."

"I hope so."

"It is so, Carmine. You're off the hook. And the FBI has a sterling record when it comes to protecting citizens who help...."

Carmine hung up the phone, cutting off Oberlin's earnest spiel. He dropped in another dime and dialed his wife. He never shared details of his business with her, but she'd noticed how jumpy he'd been the past several days whenever she asked how things were going at work.

"Hey Lore, it's me. I'm coming home early tonight. We'll go to the Shore diner, okay?" He screwed up his eyes and pressed the phone closer to his ear. "What? I can't hear you. What's all that static?"

"...working on the line outside..."

"What? They're working on the phone line?"

"Yes..." The rest of his wife's response was drowned out.

"Okay, okay. See you later." Carmine hung up, checked the coin return, then got back in his car and drove off.

Outside the Rizzo house, Benny C., dressed in a lineman's uniform, climbed down the telephone pole, tossed his tool belt into the back of a panel truck and waved good-bye to Lorena R. who was watching him from the kitchen window.

8

"Let's go everybody!" Sandra B. yelled up the stairs. "Movie starts in half an hour!" Sandra was taking her children to a double feature horror movie at the local theatre. She did not like horror, but there was that, or cartoons, at four in the afternoon.

"This is so bogus!" complained Clara, tripping down the stairs. "Why can't I stay home?"

"Because," shrieked Sandra, "this is a family outing and we're going to have a good time! Now get in the car!" She looked up the staircase. "Where's your brother?"

"Probably with his girlfriend."

Sandra tapped the banister menacingly. "What girlfriend?"

"Who do you think, mom? Lisa Forte."

Sandra stomped out to the car with Clara following at a distance. Billy was already waiting in the driver's seat. He grinned at his mother. "I'm driving, okay?"

"Not today—I'm too aggravated!"

"You're always aggravated!" moaned Billy, pulling his set of keys from the ignition and slipping them back into his jeans. He slid into the passenger seat and watched his mother get in and slide to within an inch of the steering column. "C'mon, mom," he said gently, as if trying to calm a spooked horse. "I need the practice. My road test is next week."

Sandra hesitated, then said, "Okay, okay!" and got out of the car. She walked around to the passenger side while Billy slipped behind the wheel with a victorious grin.

"Thanks, mom," he said.

"Yeah, yeah," said Sandra. She watched her son reset the seat and the mirrors, admiring his profile, youth and beauty, oblivious to the fact that Clara had just dragged herself into the back seat.

"Clara! Let's go!" She bellowed at the house.

"I'm already here!" exclaimed Clara from the back seat, causing Sandra B. to clutch at her heart dramatically.

"Don't sneak around like that, Clara!"

"Sneak around? Jeez, mom!"

"And don't say Jeez!"

Clara slammed the door and Sandra turned her attention back to her son. "You know," she said. "I heard a rumor about Lisa Forte. And I think it's something you should know." She glanced at Clara, then leaned over and whispered in Billy's ear.

"That's a lie," he said with a smirk. "And anyway, how would you know?"

"It's a mother's business to know these things."

Clara said, "What things?" But no one was paying attention.

At four o'clock sharp, Benny Cataldo opened the sliding glass door to the family room of the Benigno home and slipped inside. He'd watched Sandra and the two children drive away and waited twenty minutes, listening for voices and peering through ground floor windows for signs of movement. It wasn't easy to conceal himself in the backyard. By its very design there was no shrubbery for cover, no shed, no place for anyone to hide. The nearest neighbor was four hundred feet away, and that house was all but obscured by trees and shrubs.

He went immediately to the kitchen because that's where Sandra claimed to have heard the voice. After an expert scan of the room he went directly to the spot where he, himself, would have rigged a bug, or transmitter, along the metal housing of the light fixture hanging over the kitchen table. He stepped up on a chair and felt along the inside edge until he felt the familiar plastic casing expertly glued to the inside rim.

He had found the kitchen bug and was sure the rest of the house would be similarly equipped. What he needed to find now was the receiver, because that's what would have enabled Sandra to overhear a conversation taking place in another room.

Benny C. already knew that this was the handiwork of young Billy Benigno, the kid always asking him questions about eavesdropping devices at the Forte house—when he got tired of ogling Lisa. He went upstairs, picked the lock to the first door then closed it again at the first sign of a stuffed animal. He went into the room at the end of the hallway, which looked like prime real estate befitting the male child of an Italian American family, and picked his way in. He started with the desk drawers and hit paydirt immediately. A transistor radio, reconfigured as a receiver in just the manner Benny had taught him, was in the top drawer.

He took it downstairs, pressed the "kitchen" toggle and set it on the counter. "Testing…testing," he said, and sure enough his voice came through clearly on the receiver. Whatever Sandra had heard, she heard through this device, which Billy had left in the kitchen and forgotten about.

Benny descended the basement steps and walked through the lower level to the door with the keypad. He punched in the number Oberlin had supplied and walked into the Benigno Family meeting room. He played his hunch again and crawled under the conference table, smiling when he saw another bug expertly installed. *That kid's got real talent*, Benny thought, and he sat there admiring his protégé until he heard footsteps on the basement steps. Someone was coming down.

He scrambled out from under the massive table and headed for the small panel at the far end of the room. He pressed the door at knee height and slipped into the narrow passageway, following it to its end, beneath the woods in the Benigno backyard. He easily turned the hatch cover handle and pushed. The hatch did not budge. He worked at the hatch for ten minutes, checking the handle position, pressing his shoulders against the metal and repeating the same process until his bruised shoulders and aching arms refused to cooperate.

A wave of panic washed over him, then receded as he reasoned to himself. He would wait. He would go back to the interior door and listen.

When all was clear he would go back the way he got in. The only possible complication would be if someone decided to use the tunnel, and he considered that a very long shot indeed.

He did not consider the possibility that he would be stuck in the tunnel for a very long time. The hatch in the woods was covered by a fallen tree, and Oberlin had neglected to mention how to open the door leading back to the conference room from the side he was on.

9

The Benigno conference bunker had not been used for nearly a year, ever since a member of Victor' retinue had discovered an earlier eavesdropping attempt by the young bugster, Billy. Victor had determined, logically enough, that it had been an FBI bug, and in the first gangland hit ever ordered on an inanimate object, he had it destroyed utterly and ceremonially, after deriding its crude design and obvious placement. In some ways, young Billy had done the FBI a favor by making its agents appear incompetent, and thereby lowering the bar for any future government-sanctioned attempts at eavesdropping—if the Feds should ever locate the elusive bunker, and were then able to present probable cause for a wiretap or bug.

Seven Parkview Drive was a boxy, two story, stuccoed affair at the end of a cul de sac. There was one road in and the same road out. Constructed from plans that Victor himself had designed, the house was a veritable fortress. Every peril was considered. In order to elude the grasp of a six-foot assassin, the first floor windows were set eight feet above ground level. To stymie a drive-by shooting, the windows as well as the patio doors were triple-pane bullet resistant. For protection against ambush, the foundation walls were naked, with no shrubs or greenery of any kind that might provide a hiding place. To ensure an unobstructed view of the grounds, and of anyone coming or going, the sloping lawn was manicured, even in the dead of winter. Where the grass ended, concrete patios took over.

In these ways—some trivial, some not—the Benigno house distinguished itself from the homogeneous design elements of the

41

adjacent properties, but no complaints had ever been lodged with the neighborhood HOA.

It was late in the evening when the Forte Captains began their staggered arrival to this suburban Westchester home.

Every three minutes, a black Cadillac or Lincoln Town Car pulled up to the curb and deposited a Forte Captain, who was escorted to the rear of the house by a Benigno soldier. Here the Captain was handed off to another soldier who escorted him inside and downstairs to the basement. Within thirty minutes, after a thorough weapons check—and a strip search for potential wired informants—the six Forte Captains stood quietly around the conference table, dark-suited, clean shaven, waiting for their leader.

Both bosses entered the room together, a shared joke apparent in their beaming bonhomie. No sooner had they cleared the doorway, when a stream of Benigno soldiers—the same men who had escorted Dante and his captains into the house and relieved them of their weapons—flowed inside. They stood behind chairs to each side of Victor's chair at the head of the table. Victor motioned for Dante to take the other head, and as they sat down the rest of the men followed.

Dante's smile evaporated as he looked around the table. The ill-fitting suits, diamond pinky rings, ruddy faces from a recent shave, the scent of Old Spice mingled with testosterone—it looked like a gathering of thugs. And there was something else about the scene that bothered him. Lisa used to read Highlights for Children in Dr. Goldenberg's waiting room. Her favorite section depicted a scene—at the library, at the supermarket, at the beach, etc.—with a number of incongruous details the reader was asked to identify. Maybe a cow popped out of a cuckoo clock, or a boat sailed along a highway. It was called *What's Wrong With This Picture*, and this is what Dante was thinking as he assessed the Benigno crew.

He felt the heat rise in his face when he realized that none of the men surrounding Victor were captains. They were soldiers, and they were sitting in, *above their pay grade*, with captains from a rival family. This was a serious breach of protocol, an insult of the highest order.

It was also a thinly veiled threat.

There were no papers in the room, no agenda, memoranda, flip charts, flow charts, no hard copy record of this or any other meeting. Strategy and detail were stored in Victor Benigno's head. Persuasion was holstered under his jacket, and in the pockets of these six soldiers who stared down the table at the enemy, bodies tense, right hands flexing nervously. Forte's six captains, completely unarmed, were deer caught in the headlights—confused, disoriented, not knowing which way to turn, and getting no signal from their Capo. For Victor Benigno this was just one more in a lifetime of smart moves, the reason he was Capo di Tutti Capi, while Dante, once again, was caught with his pants down.

Victor put his elbows on the table and made a finger bridge, as if in prayer. "Let me begin by welcoming Mr. Dante Forte and his esteemed captains to this informal sit down." He waited until Dante opened his mouth to speak before continuing, "And allow me to express regrets on behalf of my own Captains that they were indisposed and unable to make this meeting. As you can see I was able to fill in. No point in letting all these chairs go to waste." He smiled and his jaw jutted forward, like a barracuda.

The hair on Dante's neck stood at attention. He floated his hands, palms down, over the table, as if this motion alone would be enough to stem the rising sense of betrayal building among his men. From the chair to Victor's right, his youngest and newest Captain, Chaz Pettini, called out, "What are you trying to pull?" He had his hand on the table, ready to push up from his chair, when Dante reached over and put a hand on his forearm. He settled back into his seat and yanked his arm away angrily. "If you don't have the balls to ask this thug, as you call him, why his goons are here armed to the teeth in an executive meeting, then I will."

"Chaz, please. I'm sure our host will explain," said Dante, eyes darting nervously from Chaz to Victor.

"I'll do better than that. I'll demonstrate." Victor reached into his breast pocket, and the Forte Captains ducked under the table. They emerged slowly when they saw that Victor had pulled out a fat cigar stump. He lit it, and exhaled toward the ceiling, watching the curl of smoke for several long seconds before turning to the soldier on his right. Victor nodded. In one smooth motion the soldier pulled out a gun, screwed on a silencer and took aim at Chaz Pettini.

"No!" Dante cried out. His hands shook as he raised them in protest. "You've made your point!"

"Not yet." Victor's eyebrow moved almost imperceptibly. The bullet hit Pettini in the throat and lodged in his windpipe. He seemed surprised at first, and wheezed out a "What the fuck." Then he turned to Dante in horror, clutching at his neck, but Dante moved away reflexively as the next shot hit Pettini in the back of the head. This time Pettini got to his feet and lunged toward his attacker, catching one foot on the table leg.

"Christ! Hit him again!"

The third bullet hit Pettini in the eye. He wavered, knees locked, then crumpled to the floor at Victor's feet like a marionette. Dante looked quizzically at Victor Benigno, then fixed his gaze on the lifeless body and mutilated head of his young captain. For a long moment no one moved. Dante raised his head slowly, as if lifting a great weight, and looked across the table at Victor Benigno. "Why?" was the only word he could find.

"Why?" The Boss squinted at this stupid question. "He was a slacker, Victor. Hasn't run a decent counterfeit business for years."

"Why would you care?" said Dante carefully. "He worked for *me*."

Victor' lips turned up in a smile. His eyes remained hard black stones. "I care, Victor, because as of tomorrow he would have been working for *me*." Victor watched impassively as Dante's face turned pink with muted rage. This Capo had just witnessed the murder of one of his captains by a rival family—in front of his own organization—and his only response was, *why?* He had no use for this impotent half-a-fag who had neglected his own organization and ran it into the ground by giving men like Pettini too much freedom. What he would not tell Dante—not tonight in front of the others—was that Pettini had been working for the Feds for the past two years. And for the past two years the Forte businesses had been raided and shut down, one after the other. Dante, with his head up his behind, had never suspected one of his hand picked captains of being a rat. Worse still, he never suspected his own sound-man, Benny C., of being a mole for Victor, his fiercest rival.

When you are a Boss, it pays to know these things.

He looked at each of Dante's captains in turn. *Stunads*, all of them. How could they not know this day was coming. "As for the rest of you," he said, addressing the Forte captains, "you are now on the Benigno payroll, with all the opportunities and obligations that this new status entails." He added, "I hope there are no questions." Two Benigno soldiers put their guns on the table. There were no questions.

He turned to Dante. "As of tomorrow you will be my partner—but you will be a silent partner, so I'll give you one last opportunity to address these *stunads*. Do you have anything to say?"

The flush faded from Dante's face as newfound confidence surged through his breast. He stood slowly and addressed the expectant faces of his crumbling organization. "Yes, I do have something to say. Please note that *Stunad* is a slang term used only by the unwashed masses." He glared at Victor, and at each Benigno soldier in turn. "The correct word, meaning tone-deaf, is stonato. S-T-O-N-A-T-O, for those of you who know how to spell."

"I heard gunshots, Billy. Those were gunshots!" Lisa Dante, dressed in ski jacket and boots over her pajamas, wrung her hands and watched Billy Benigno's face with wild eyes, waiting for his response. "Billy!" she urged in a low, hoarse whisper. "Were they gunshots?"

They were standing in the kitchen where Billy had invited Lisa for a live demonstration of his eavesdropping handiwork. "No. A gunshot is much louder." He knew about silencers but did not want to completely spoil what was supposed to have been a romantic evening, made even more exciting by the possibility of being caught. "They were just thumps. Someone falling against the wall, most likely."

Lisa pretended to be reassured, and the two teenagers resumed their positions, crouched on the kitchen floor with Billy's receiver between their heads. The scent of Lisa's herbal shampoo made him heady and horny. Her hair, the red rubber boots, the panda pajamas—all of it was immensely arousing to the sixteen year-old, and he wished they could stay that way forever.

Lisa, who'd been awakened by pebbles tossed at her bedroom window, had looked down at the handsome Billy and imagined him as her knight in shining silver parka, here to rescue her from Castle Keep. She'd felt a familiar tickle in her belly as she climbed down the trellis into foot-deep snow.

"Do you think this is something important that we shouldn't be listening to?" said Lisa, pulling the receiver closer to her ear.

Her naivete, whether real or feigned, gave Billy an overwhelming urge to shelter and protect the object of his desires. Also, he was relieved to see that he was the smarter of the two. Of course it was important! They had overheard plans for a major shift in Family structure, information that only the most highly placed and well-connected members of the Families would know, and all of this had been made possible by Billy's keen interest in Benny C.'s work. Benny knew that information was the best business of all. It cost nothing, if you knew how to steal it, and you could sell it for whatever price you wanted, as long as someone needed it badly enough.

Lisa set the receiver down on the floor and gazed into Billy's clear hazel eyes. "I feel closer to you now, Billy, as if we're related."

"Call me Bill. Just Bill." He leaned in but before their lips touched, the shuffling of chairs screeched on the small receiver. "Shit!" Lisa scrambled to her feet and ran out the kitchen door. Billy bounded up the stairs to his bedroom, heart pounding, exquisitely aware of the enemy's proximity on the staircase below.

Lisa was halfway to the end of the property line just as four men came out of the house, onto the back patio. There was nowhere to hide, no trees or shrubs or even a shed to step behind. She stood motionless on the snow covered lawn, silhouetted against the far off woods, cursing her red boots. But as long as she remained still her form would merge with the dark.

She heard a car drive up, saw the headlights on the side of the house, near the garage. The men walked around the corner of the house to the garage and came back carrying what looked like a tree limb, but was in fact a nine by twelve foot bolt of carpet. They marched it sideways into the house.

Lisa ran for the tree-line and emerged in the adjacent cul-de-sac. The air was frigid and still as the stars. She crossed her arms over her chest and pulled the ski jacket tightly to her body, pretending she was wrapped in the arms of Billy Benigno.

Ten feet away from the conference table, behind a wood-paneled door in a mostly sound proof tunnel, Benny C. lay flat on his back, oblivious to the cold blooded and messy execution of Chaz Pettini.

But Benny had his own problems now and they were about to get worse. Up to now, he'd been incredibly lucky. He'd been able to tolerate three days without food because fear of being discovered by Victor and his goons—and imagining all the ways he could be executed—had dulled his appetite. He was smart enough to know that he would not survive in the cold tunnel more than three days without water—but in a stroke of luck, he'd stumbled upon a case of Bolla Soave, with which he had been hydrating himself on an empty stomach. As a result, although things were certainly bad, they didn't *feel* so bad.

In fact, under different circumstances things could have been very good, and very profitable, and if he weren't trapped in this shithole, he mused ruefully, he'd be a rich man.

Because along with the case of Bolla wine, Benny had found an egg crate filled with black and white composition books. He'd opened one, glanced at the childlike scrawling and tossed it back in the pile, assuming it belonged to the Benigno kids. But hours later boredom got the better of him and he took a closer look.

These were, in fact, bookies' books, hundreds of gambling records with names and dollar amounts paid, due and—underlined in red—overdue. He knew some of the debtors, and was mildly surprised to see, represented in the sloppy columns, some fine upstanding citizens, including his own city councilman, a circuit court judge, and several New York City cops. But it was finding Ken Schneider's name on the list that actually made Benny smile. Alongside the FBI boss' name it said "paid in full."

The obvious irony of his find, a federal law enforcement official as Mob patron, did not register on Benny. Because he was a practical man, and a product—as well as perpetuator— of the dark side of humanity, Benny's thoughts were more literal. *Paid in full my ass!* He flipped through the book, tearing out every page with Schneider's name—twelve in all, spanning five years. Then he checked the other books and pulled out more pages, these dating back nine years. With these records he would squeeze the FBI boss, wring him dry.

Benny tallied up the ways he would score with all the information he now possessed—as soon as he got himself out of this hellhole. Benny knew that Carmine's wife was the beneficiary of a sizable life insurance policy that his mother-in-law had talked Carmine into buying. He also knew that Carmine's wife was having an affair, so he'd be in line for a chunk of that payout just for keeping his mouth shut. Every which-way he turned, Benny could not lose. Information was twice as profitable when you worked both sides against the middle.

These were pleasant musings, and they helped anchor Benny to the land of the living, a land of hope, and his thoughts turned to *Benny C's Escape and Retribution*: If Victor's goons came into the tunnel, maybe to get the books, or the wine, Benny would press himself flat against the wall so he'd be behind the door when they opened it. Then, as soon as they walked inside he'd run out and slam the door shut in their faces.

He would trade places with them. Benny C. would be free and the Benigno goons—maybe even Victor—would be trapped inside. They would die instead of Benny. He reached for two bottles of the remaining wine and held them close to his chest. If he escaped, he'd take these with him.

For as long as he could remember, nobody ever gave anything to Benny Cataldo. And now, if Benny's plan worked out, the boss and his goons would find themselves in *his* place, relying on their *own* smarts to survive. He let out a short, "heh," deriding their efforts in advance, should this fever dream ever take flight.

10

"Yes. I have a contact at INS," said Schneider. He wheeled around in his chair and threw a dart at his wife's needlepoint, which now hung behind his office door. "However," he said, swiveling back, "I would need a really good reason to call in a favor right now." He watched Oberlin knit his eyebrows in a show of meaningful cogitation. "Do you have a really good reason for me, Agent Oberlin?"

Instead of saying what he felt—that he had made a promise to an informant—Oberlin said mildly, "This individual can help you win, Ken."

"Win?"

"Yes, win. I know you're wagering on the outcome of this OC Squad strategy..."

"You're nuts."

"C'mon, Ken. You bet on everything."

"How do you know that?"

"Every time you win you take us out for beers."

"Nothing wrong with it, you know."

"Never said there was...except, perhaps, a conflict of interest."

Schneider studied Oberlin for a few seconds before breaking into a triumphant grin. "You're absolutely right, Mark. And there certainly would be a conflict of interest if I did certain unprofessional things, like playing favorites in allocating resources, or—oh, I don't know—like calling in a favor from the INS."

"So, you won't do it."

"No."

"Guess I shouldn't have brought up the gambling..."

"Wouldn't have made the slightest bit of difference."

Oberlin headed for the door. "Hey, Mark," called Schneider. "Which team do you think I'm betting on, anyway?"

Oberlin gave a non-committal shrug. He figured Schneider was all in for Tommy D'Angelo, partly because Tommy was the best at what he did. Mostly, though, he knew that Schneider had a profound hatred of Victor Benigno and wanted him to be the first to fall. "I hope you get what you want," Oberlin replied, and left the office.

Oberlin and Semple sat caddy-cornered at the bar of a local pub. "Benny is sweeping the Benigno house," said Oberlin, softly. "If he finds anything, I'd say the Sandra story is actionable."

Hayford eyed the bartender, waited for him to move away. "Who'd have thought, a Forte informant inside the Benigno walls. How did you arrange it?"

"Sandra. She wants it done."

"Pretty risky for her."

"She's protecting her son. In the animal kingdom mothers kill to protect their children."

"I guess. But don't some mothers eat their young?"

"Meaning?"

"Oh, I don't know. Could be a setup. Maybe the real deal will be taking place miles away and we have all our resources at the wrong spot."

"No," replied Oberlin emphatically. "That makes no sense. They would keep the whole operation under wraps in that case."

Semple thought for a moment. "Why is Benny going along with this? He's a dead man if the timing is even slightly off."

"I promised I'd help his relative pass a marriage interview with the INS. The problem is," he continued, "I was counting on Schneider's in with the agency and he won't play ball."

"Not to worry. I have a friend or two over there."

"Perfect!" Oberlin raised his glass to toast his partner then downed the shot of bourbon and smiled broadly, pleased with himself for managing to cover all bases and all promises made in connection with this project. It was tempting to wonder what could possibly go wrong, but it was not in his character to do so.

11

"This is a progress meeting, people. If you haven't made any, you're excused." Ken Schneider did an eyeball sweep of the assembled agents. Some were attentive, a few worked hastily on overdue reports, and at least one was gently snoring in the back of the room. Schneider took aim with his inter-office directory and grazed the top of the sleeping agent's head. "Go home and get some rest, Dawson." The agent gathered his things and walked past his colleagues, who shook their heads and snickered like schoolboys. "I don't know what the rest of you find so amusing," said Schneider. "Agent Dawson just busted up the largest bookmaking operation in the five boroughs." A vigorous round of applause followed Agent Dawson to the door.

"I want to talk about the Italian American Anti-Defamation demonstration that took place in the lobby of this building on Tuesday afternoon. As most of you know, three Con Edison workers were hospitalized in attacks that were meant for you—or more specifically, for members of the FBI's Benigno squad."

"We made two arrests," Tommy D'Angelo called out.

"Three is not enough."

"I said 'two' arrests."

"There's nothing wrong with my hearing," replied Schneider. He cupped his hands behind his large ears and the room broke into laughter. "I want to know why there were only three attacks?"

"There were only three Con Ed workers," said someone.

Schneider let out a breath and shook his head despairingly. "Benigno's goons were not going after the Electric Company, people. They thought they were attacking undercover agents. There were twenty of us in the office that day. It could have turned into a riot." He turned to D'Angelo. "And then, Agent D'Angelo, we could have made hundreds of arrests. Get my drift?"

D'Angelo nodded slowly and the room broke into a buzz. Mark Oberlin, who had been working on a report, put down his pen, moved his glance from Schneider to D'Angelo, and then scanned the other faces in the room. What had he missed? Was Schneider encouraging his agents to incite a riot? He smiled at himself and went back to his paperwork.

"We have work to do," Schneider announced, signaling an end to the meeting. He added, "Oberlin and D'Angelo, stick around."

The agents went back to their work. From opposite corners of the room Oberlin and D'Angelo approached Schneider, who was sitting on the edge of a desk, slowly picking through the contents of a thick pendoflex file. "So, gentlemen. I trust you've found a solution to the Benigno problem, i.e. credible evidence of a pending criminal situation."

D'Angelo shot Oberlin a glance, which Oberlin interpreted as license to speak first. "I'm on it, Ken. Tom was kind enough to refer a highly placed informant to me, and I'm working on a strategic response. Would you care to know the details?"

"No details," Schneider said sharply. "That's what you were hired for. I'm the big picture guy, remember?" He glanced at Tommy D'Angelo, who had been pacing the small space intently, as if waiting for the men's room to free up. "Glad to see you're so anxious to get to work, D'Angelo. I want you to partner with Agent Oberlin. Your squads will work Benigno together." D'Angelo opened his mouth to speak but Schneider cut him off, adding, "You, Agent D'Angelo, will take the lead."

D'Angelo clicked his heels together and saluted. "Will do."

Schneider closed his office door. He picked up his phone, started to dial, then put it down. He grabbed his jacket and left the office, telling his secretary he would be gone for an hour.

He rode the subway to Canal Street and walked three blocks crosstown to Sal's Ocean Produce, a dilapidated storefront on the corner, which was very much in keeping with the no frills tone of the lower east side neighborhood. The sign, in the seafaring style, was so weathered as to be illegible, but even on this freezing January day patrons could find it by smell alone.

The battered wooden door opened with a delicate tinkle. Behind a counter covered in fish slime, three hundred pound Sal Palomino greeted him with a deeply dimpled dough-boy smile. "Kenny boy. What can I do for you?"

Schneider glanced around. The door to the back room was open and they seemed to be alone. "I want the books, Sal."

Palomino feigned surprise, quickly followed by an approximation of hurt. "Kenny, Kenny. I'm out of the business. You know that." He cocked his enormous head to one side and held his fish covered hands palms up. "And so are you, my frirend! You settled your IOU's. As far as Victor is concerned, everyone's square. Am I right, or am I right?"

Schneider spoke in a low monotone, as if this fish monger was not worthy of any declarative effort. "This was the deal. I pay off all debts. You provide me with the books. I keep any pages with my name on them."

"Yeah, well, funny thing." Palomino mimicked Schneider's clipped delivery. "Those books don't exist. I got everything right up here." He tapped the side of his head with a slimy finger. A wad of fish viscera stuck to his hair.

"I want those books, Sal."

"Are you calling me a liar, Agent Schneider?" Palomino forced a half-moon smile. He picked up a piece of fish and Ken ducked, but instead of flinging it Palomino dangled it daintily by the tail. "Hey, how about a nice piece of cod to take home to the little lady."

Schneider backed out of the shop and the door jangled loudly when he slammed it shut.

12

At lunchtime the following day Mark Oberlin broke the news to his partner that they would be joining the Benigno squad. Hayford Semple was not happy with this new arrangement. "I've got three informants working inside Forte right now. One of them is my TEI, went in as a captain with a nice forgery business, you know, stock certificates, CD's, all types of financial instruments."

"Looks like forgery will have to wait," Oberlin replied.

Hay smiled and gave Oberlin a hard pat on the back. "Well now, that's nice work, Mark. So you found the legs on that Sandra B. story after all."

"No, not really. I'm still looking for those."

"So why the switch?"

Oberlin shrugged. "Schneider wants it that way. I'm not sure why. Maybe he wants to take them down one by one starting from the top."

Hay laughed. "Time for another reorganization. Our new, improved OC *squad* concept lasted what – three days?"

They entered Central Park at 67th Street, bought a couple of Tabs and four Sabrett hotdogs from the first vendor they saw, and settled down for a lap lunch on the cold wooden planks of a bench.

Oberlin contemplated the austere beauty of Central Park in January. If you had to be a tree, this was the place to be one, instead of languishing in a tiny plot along a fume choked side street, barraged with dog piss, stunted and bent under the snow. Not that trees had the choice.

"Trees are stuck," he said. "Imagine not being able to move to a bigger plot, or a better neighborhood. I mean, not being able to *move*, Hay."

"Of course they move. They grow toward the sun."

"Phototropism is not upward mobility."

"In the plant kingdom that's exactly what it is. In fact, there's no finer example of upward mobility." Hay chewed the last of his lunch. "Anyway, upward mobility is bullshit."

"How so?"

"It's really just sideways mobility, isn't it? We confuse movement with progress, so we keep on running, all our lives. And because the world is round, we're just chasing our tails."

"We're chasing the bad guys."

"Right. And sometimes we *are* the bad guys."

Oberlin saw the cloud of depression settle over his partner's face. Depression was the reason for his drinking problem, and that problem was the proximate cause of his divorce. Hayford Semple needed something to occupy his mind, to glue it in place for a while and keep it from its habitual tangential wanderings. At the risk of proving Hay's point about sideways mobility, Oberlin suggested they get back to work.

Semple jumped up from the bench as if he had a rocket in his pants. "Only if you tell me that Benny the Bug has located the source of the late night voices, and that we can assume with a high degree of confidence that Sandra B.'s story is real."

Standing up slowly, Oberlin replied, "I can confidently give that statement a provisional yes."

"Why provisional?"

"I haven't debriefed my source."

"Benny? Why not?"

"He never showed up—but I'm not worried. We have a three-day-gap understanding. If he doesn't show up, it means someone's on his tail and he's laying low."

"What if he doesn't show up after three days?"

"I go after him. Either he's in trouble, or he's switched sides. I'm responsible for him, either way."

"How many days is it now?"

Oberlin cleared his throat. "Three."

"What are you waiting for, Mark?" Hayford Semple caught his

partner's eyes and waited for an answer. "He went into the Benigno house, right?"

"Yes."

"So you don't know if he even came out."

"Of course he's out," said Oberlin uneasily. "He's okay or I would have heard otherwise."

"What are you going to tell D'Angelo—" Semple looked at his watch—"in about twenty minutes from now?"

"Same thing I just told you. We have a probable actionable event Friday afternoon at a car dealership. I am expecting corroboration of the source's intelligence at any time."

"Perfect. I can just hear D'Angelo's response to that."

At the FBI office Tommy D'Angelo and three of his squad members were already seated at the conference table. Agent Marino, recently transferred from the Boston office, tapped his pencil obsessively on his blank white pad.

"Do you mind," said D'Angelo, looking at the pencil, then working his way up to Marino's face. "That's really annoying."

Marino placed the pencil horizontally across the top edge of his pad. "This whole assignment is annoying. I've got some very valuable informants inside Forte. What am I supposed to tell them?"

"You tell them nothing," D'Angelo replied. "We use them, remember? Not the other way around. There's no reason for them to know our m.o."

"We don't even know our m.o. Schneider keeps changing it."

Oberlin and Semple entered the room. Weights shifted, chairs moved and two spaces opened up at the end of the table opposite Tommy D'Angelo.

"Good afternoon, gentlemen," said Oberlin amiably. "I trust Agent D'Angelo has explained why agents from the Benigno squad have joined you at this meeting."

"Yeah," said Ryan. "We're here to double-team the Benigno Family."

"Well, yes," replied Oberlin. "But more specifically, we need to plan a response to—" he looked over at Semple—"a probable actionable event Friday afternoon at…a car dealership. Details pending."

D'Angelo added, "We'll proceed without a Title Three."

The mood in the room lightened. Marino saluted with his right hand and gave D'Angelo the high sign with his left, under the table. A Title Three wiretap would require a detailed description of why a wiretap was necessary, instead of relying on informant interviews. The original informant would have to be proven unreliable, in an affidavit supported by a detailed criminal records search and retrieval, all of which would need to be documented in the report. This was a numbingly tedious assignment, and there was not enough time to get it done.

When the room cleared out D'Angelo followed Oberlin to the door. "You never started a Title Three, Mark. Your source must be pretty reliable."

"Very reliable."

"But you won't tell me who it is."

"You know I can't do that. I'd never ask you to divulge a source."

D'Angelo smirked. "Mark, as far as I'm concerned, without a Title Three, this is only a *possible* actionable event. It could be a huge waste of the Bureau's time and resources. Not to mention my own." He continued, "By the way, I only gave you Carmine because I knew he had nothing. So if you're relying on his intel you're more out of touch than he is."

Oberlin said evenly, "You didn't give me Carmine. I took him because he thought he was a dead man."

"I see. You're just trying to save a rat with the hinkies—which, by the way, makes him completely unreliable."

"First of all, I never said Carmine was my source. Secondly, I always try to keep the body count as low as possible. I don't like them any more than you do, Tom. But I don't sabotage them for sport."

"What about revenge?"

"It's never crossed my mind."

D'Angelo held Oberlin's eye. "C'mon, Mark. Haven't you ever had the urge to throw a wiseguy under a bus?"

"Never."

D'Angelo laughed. "You're full of shit. Everyone working OC has that urge. I'm the only one honest enough to admit it." On his way to the door he added, "And before you judge me, Mark, let's count the ways you bend the rules to get what you want."

Oberlin watched D'Angelo leave the room and pull the door closed hard, as if to trap this remark inside for Oberlin to stew in.

But D'Angelo's point was well taken. Oberlin had not only bent the rules, he had broken laws, not the least of which was aiding and abetting the breaking, entering and eavesdropping activity of his own informant, Benny Cataldo. The inevitable inquisition following the auto/art bust, would go something like this:

"Agent Oberlin, why did you ignore procedure and neglect to order a Title 3 Wiretap on the Benigno home?"

"Why? To circumvent the bureaucracy."

"We are a Bureau, Agent Oberlin. Bureaucracy is our stock-in-trade."

"And to protect my witness."

"The Justice Department takes care of witnesses. Do you intend to circumvent WITSEC?

"Is WITSEC a bureaucracy?"

And so on.

13

The Fix was a small repair shop on Delancey Street in lower Manhattan, wedged between Stella Pizza and a newspaper kiosk. At four p.m. two men in ski parkas huddled under a street lamp. They hunched their shoulders against the cold while their vapor-streams of epithets, directed at the absent shopkeeper, filled the air.

"Three days of this bullshit, man," said one. He had a crusty beard and tattered ski cap, and could have been sixteen or sixty.

"I'm gonna walk," said the other. He pulled a heavy backpack from between his legs and eased it onto his shoulders.

"You crazy? You'll get your balls ripped off."

"You gonna report me?"

They looked up and down the avenue. The newspaper kiosk was busy, people dropping a nickel on the counter for a Daily News and going about their business. "Three days. He must be dead, man."

"Maybe he's taking a vacation."

"With all the coin still on the street? No way."

The coin in question consisted of tens of thousands of nickels, dimes and quarters that these men, and hundreds of others like them, rifled from phone booths throughout the city, an activity that the LCN—always sniffing around for business opportunities with good cash flow—took over from the hippies and the druggies. Most nights Benny C. took in about twenty-five hundred. He reported one thousand to his Forte crew boss, who collected five hundred dollars. The men who supplied the coin were not smart enough to pull the same scam on Benny. They paid him for the privilege of being able to steal without interference from the Mob, by handing over all but a small portion of the take.

The repair shop was a minimally-staged front. There was a toaster on a shelf near the window, sandwiched between an eighteen inch Zenith television and a record player. People walked in with broken gadgets, but Benny made sure his prices were the highest in the neighborhood. His legitimate business was slow, which was just the way he liked it.

The men hitched their backpacks onto their shoulders and walked down Delancey toward the Williamsburg Bridge. Suddenly, when a dark Ford Falcon rolled up along the curb beside them, they pinned their gaze to the sidewalk and stepped up their pace.

"Dump the pack and run," said one.

"Fuck you," said the other. He took off across Hester Street and disappeared down an alley. The remaining coin thief watched the Ford Falcon carefully insert itself at the curb in a perfect parallel park. He decided there was nothing to fear from its driver.

"Excuse me," said a friendly voice from the passenger window. "I'm looking for Benny C."

"The Fix, down the street."

"I know. I was there earlier but he doesn't seem to be in."

The man shrugged. "Can't help you."

Agent Oberlin got out of the car and walked around to the sidewalk showing a full-tooth smile to the tattered young man with the heavy backpack.

"So you know Benny," said Oberlin.

"Benny repairs my stuff," the man replied, tightening his grip on the pack.

"I see," said Oberlin. The homeless did not generally possess items that would need repair. But Oberlin was fully aware of Benny's coin franchise—he could count to the penny the contents of this man's backpack—and never interfered. This was Benny's compensation for becoming a Forte family informant. Oberlin said carefully, "How long has the shop been closed?"

The backpacker replied, "How the fuck should I know."

He sprinted across the street. Oberlin watched him go, feeling helpless and stupid in the middle of the sidewalk. It was clear to him that Benny had not come back from his mission. There was no way he would have abandoned his business.

He walked three blocks to a pay phone, dropped a dime and dialed the Benigno home.

"Mom! It's for you."

Billy held the phone out and Sandra mouthed the words *who is it?*

"He didn't say."

Didn't you ask? She mouthed fiercely, her lips contorting like rubber bands.

Billy watched her and mouthed *What?*

"Just give me the phone," she snarled, snatching the handset. When the cord would not stretch far enough she picked up the entire princess phone and carried it around the corner into the hallway. "Who's calling?"

"Mark Oberlin."

"Are you out of your mind? Calling me at home!" she wheezed into the receiver.

"Who is it, mom?" called Billy.

"My Travel Agent!" she aimed her voice toward the kitchen.

"Can I take the car out? I need driving practice."

"Don't go near the car!" She waited until she heard her son stomp away on heavy feet. Taking a deep breath she whispered hoarsely into the phone, "What do you want?"

"It seems that we've lost track of Benny," said Oberlin lightly, trying not to frighten the woman whose home was his last known location.

"The snoop who was in my house?"

"Yes."

"Mark. What are you saying?"

"Look, Sandra, I know this will seem like a strange request—and I don't want you to be overly concerned, because in all the likelihood he is someplace else entirely, but—"

"Get to the point!"

"There is a slim possibility that Mr. Cataldo is still inside your home."

"Inside my home?" Sandra's loud cackle brought Billy's head poking around the around.

"Billy—Go do your homework!" She waited for her son to disappear, then said, "I can assure you that there is no extra person in this house."

"Have you checked?"

"If you mean have I searched my entire house for some dirty stooge that you guys lost, the answer is no."

"Would you mind checking, just in case?"

Sandra's eyes darted around in their sockets, looking for a place to land. "Do you really think…"

"No. Not really, but possibly…"

"Because it's been three days…"

"I know."

"And he's just…not here." She waited a moment and another potentially salient point popped into her head. "My husband had a meeting here last night."

Oberlin felt his neck stiffen. "Where does he hold his meetings?"

"The conference room in the lower level, but no one's allowed in there."

"So you didn't check it."

"Check it? I told you no one's allowed in there!"

"Got it," said Oberlin, without reminding her that she had allowed Benny into her house with full access to every room. "Is your husband home?"

"No."

"Would you mind going down there now?"

"Oh, Geez, I can't believe—"

"And please call me at—"

"Yeah, yeah. I know. Two one two, five three seven, zero one zero two."

63

Her eyes moved reflexively to the grandfather clock in the living room. Victor was due home in an hour. Touching the Saint Christopher medal at her neck she prayed that he would not come home early today. Then she sent a second prayer requesting that he not come home at all.

"Don't ever call me here again," she said to Oberlin, her voice shaking. "You'll get me *and* my son killed!" She hung up and carried the phone back to the kitchen. Satisfied that Clara and Billy were tucked away in their rooms, she pulled off her shoes and went downstairs. She clicked on the wall switch and a soft glow filled the space, just enough light to illuminate the obvious while leaving potential problems undisturbed. She walked through the rooms, scanning the floor for an irregular shape, a breach in a shadow that a body might make. She stopped at the conference room, hesitated, then punched in the code and opened the door to a distinctive smell. It was the primal scent of men: a musky keynote with undertones of power and sex, and a grace note of fear.

The table top was clear, the chairs neatly aligned.

Sandra backed out of the room and closed the door. She hurried upstairs, satisfied that there was no body, dead or otherwise, lurking in her home. And she was beginning to question her choice of Agent Oberlin. "Billy, Clara!" she called up the stairs. "I'm going over to Aunt Ginni's for canasta." And for a shot or two of Southern Comfort, just to soothe the nerves.

Billy Benigno. Only son of Victor Benigno, Cappo di tutti Cappi. Billy had no need for cheap thrills like sex and drugs to get a rush. All he had to do was *be* a Benigno. The thrills were there for the taking.

His mom had been talking to a Travel Agent? Yeah, right. Probably an FBI Agent. In a day in the life of a Mob kid there were always G-Men around. Sometimes he saw them on the road to the house, sitting in their shitty cars. He could recognize them anywhere. He wondered, vaguely, why one had called, and what he'd wanted from his mother. Good thing his father wasn't home. He'd go nuts if he knew the FBI was harassing his wife. Maybe Billy would tell him. Maybe it was his duty to report this to his father.

Billy respected his father. Victor was tough on him, but Billy knew it was for his own good, to make him understand people, and how the world worked.

"There are eight slices in a pizza," Victor had pointed out to Billy when he was still a young boy. "You never want to cut more, because then your slice gets smaller and doesn't fill you up. What you gotta do is grab another slice when no one's looking."

"What if someone sees you take it?" Billy had replied.

"Then you gotta fire them from the pizza. You know what firing means, right? Get rid of them so they can't tell on you."

"Fire them," Billy had repeated.

"And then there's even more pie for you, right?"

"Right." To a seven year-old, this logic was impeccable.

He knew that what his father did was sometimes not exactly legal, but everyone's father did illegal things, like not paying taxes or doing drugs. Even Jim Farrow's dad in the NYPD kept some of the pot from drug busts. No one knew, and no one cared. These were just ordinary people getting the most out of life.

Why should the Benigno's be any different. And as his father had said many times, why should the Benigno's not be on top of the heap, like in the Sinatra song.

But Billy had a sense of the glamour, rather than the actual fact, of Family life. Even now, as a six foot two inch, one hundred and eighty pound teenager, he was not allowed anywhere near the family business. He knew Victor would go nuts if he found out he was snooping around in his private rooms, no less wiring them for sound. But what would his father do, exactly? He wouldn't kill him, put a bullet between his eyes. He wouldn't even take a swing at him. Victor was very non-physical with him and Clara. He left all the punishments up to their mother— and she always took their side, almost no matter what—so there was never any punishment at all. Amazing, really, that they had grown up so normal.

That was the proof Billy Benigno needed that his father and mother were normal as well. This was the way Billy wanted things, so this is the way he imagined them.

And anyway, he had a really hot girlfriend, and Lisa was more or less in the same boat.

With Sandra out of the house, Clara in her room and his father not due home for an hour, Billy went downstairs to check for glitches in his electronic equipment. Maybe the Feds had traced it somehow, even though Mr. Cataldo had told him that the Feds were living in the stone ages when it came to technology. Even so, Billy carefully inspected the basement rooms for any sign of FBI tampering.

Letting himself into the conference room he went straight to the hidden doorway, this secret portal now a magnet for the teenaged Billy, who wanted another chance in the tunnel, to prove to himself that he could escape. He felt for the sweet spot with his knee, then froze. A soft moan, baby-like, came from inside. He pressed his ear to the panel and waited, holding his breath. It came again, softer, barely more than a whisper. He knew the tunnel was sound proofed, which meant the creature could be howling on the other side of the door.

Could be a raccoon trapped in there, he thought. *Could have rabies. Better leave it alone.*

A hard lump rose in Billy's throat. He knew what raccoons sounded like, and it wasn't this. There was no way an animal could have found its way in from outdoors because the hatch cover in the woods was still blocked by a tree. Whatever was in there, whatever had moaned, had entered from inside. It had to open the door and close it. It had hands.

"Billy!" Sandra's voice hit him like a pail of cold water. His father— Cappo di Tutti Cappi—was due home any minute, and Billy could find himself in a world of shit. He hurried back through the outer room, stopping at the conference table for a quick inspection of his bug. Getting down on one knee he peered underneath. It was still in place.

"Billy!"

He bounded up the stairs two at a time. No sooner had he closed the basement door than his father swept into the kitchen, like a cold wind before a squall. "Hey Billy. How's it going?" Victor's gaze dropped to his son's leg. "What's that on your knee?" he said, then turned to the fridge and pulled out two cans of beer. "Here, catch." He tossed a can but Billy was staring at the dark stain on the right knee of his khakis. The can crashed to the kitchen floor. "Sorry," Billy said quickly, picking it up.

"Don't open it. It'll go off like a bomb," said Victor. "Take another."

Victor settled onto a stool at the kitchen counter and sipped his beer. He was too big for the stool. It disappeared under his bulk, and it looked as if he was stuck directly to the pedestal, like an enormous popsicle. Billy said, "No thanks," and knew he should get out of the kitchen before the subject of his stained pants came up. But he stayed, watching his father placidly sip his beer, and stare at the can as if he had never read a Schaefer's label before. There was no other place for his father to look. The counter faced the sink, where a pasta pot was soaking in suds, and the refrigerator, which was plastered to capacity with Billy and Clara's primitive artwork, some of it five years old.

He saw his father's back swell with a deep breath, or a sigh, and he felt something strange deep down in his belly. Pity, shame, love, whatever. It was all very sad.

In the first floor powder room Sandra applied some lipstick, smoothed her hair, which looked like hay before baling, and spritzed it with Alberto VO5 Extra Hold hairspray. Like a one-woman bomb squad—on three-inch heels—she carefully picked her way into the kitchen, eyes darting left and right, sweeping for domestic landmines.

"What was that crash?" she said.

Victor had his back to them. Sandra looked Billy up and down, her eyes widening when she saw the stain.

"I dropped a beer," said Billy.

"What's for dinner?" said Clara, trudging into the kitchen. Her friend, a wispy blonde with a mouthful of crowded teeth, trailed reluctantly behind.

"Chicken," said Sandra.

"What kind?"

"With sausages."

"I hate sausages. Can Angela stay?"

In the dull afterglow of her Southern Comfort high, Sandra felt prickly with impatience. "Is it okay with you?" she said to the back of her husband's head.

"What, the kid staying for supper?" He swiveled slowly and looked at Clara's friend. "Angela means angel, you know."

Clara rolled her eyes while Angela squirmed uncomfortably under Victor's gaze. "Are you an angel, Angela?"

"I guess. Sometimes."

"Wrong answer. You gotta be dead to be an angel. That's not something you want, right Angela?"

"Da-a-a-d!" Clara screeched.

"What? I'm just giving her a logic lesson."

"Thanks a lot! Now she probably doesn't even *want* to stay." Clara looked beseechingly at her friend. "Do you?"

"I don't care." Angela wiped her nose with her sleeve. "Can I have a Kleenex?"

Ten minutes later, alone in his room, Billy pulled off his pants and examined the stain. It was the color of iron oxide from chemistry class. It could have been rust, it could have been paint, but it was neither of those things. It was dried, congealed blood.

The events came back to him in a rush—the angry voices, the short silence with a violent ending in the downstairs conference room. He and Lisa had both heard gunfire—which Billy had both pretended was something else. But someone had been shot, the same person who had moaned from inside the tunnel. He was lying in there badly wounded and waiting to die, and Billy had knelt in his blood.

He ran to the hall bathroom, locked the door and retched into the toilet until he felt empty and cold inside, and calm enough to think. Back in his room he balled up his stained pants and looked for a place to stow them. His bureau and desk drawers were no good. His mother frequently went through them. Ditto for the closet, so he shoved them under his dresser where, according to his mother, the cleaning lady never looked. He sat down at his desk, grabbed a pencil and wrote out a series of ten digit numbers. He recognized the tenth sequence as the one his mother had recited during her conversation with Agent Oberlin.

He pulled on a pair of jeans and his ski jacket, grabbed some coins from the top of his dresser and slipped quietly downstairs and out the front door. The nearest pay phone was a mile away, at a gas station on County Road 53. Billy slogged through the snow in his sneakers. His feet felt like cement stumps by the time he arrived. He pumped the coins into the change box and dialed the number pressed into his brain, dully aware that it might be after office hours at the FBI. He stamped his feet, keeping time with the rings…one…two…three…

"Mark Oberlin."

Billy found no words.

"This is Mark Oberlin…Hello?" Oberlin waited a few seconds. "Who's calling please?"

A long moment passed, then the words tumbled out. "This is Billy Benigno, Sandra's son. I was in the basement and I think I might have found something but I don't want to tell my mother because she'll go nuts and you really gotta promise me you won't tell her I called you—"

"Slow down, son." Oberlin said urgently. "Where are you calling from?"

"A gas station."

"The one on Route 53?"

"Yeah."

"Is your father home?"

69

"Yeah."

"Any chance of getting him out of the house?"

"No. Look, can't you just bust in and go downstairs?"

"Hold on, Billy. Is there an outside entrance to the basement?"

"There's the tunnel. That's where I think I heard…something."

"A tunnel?" In all the ground and aerial surveillance of the Benigno home over the past decade, there had been no evidence of a tunnel. "Where does it lead?"

"It connects with an old bomb shelter, out in the woods behind our house. But you can't get in that way. The hatch is blocked by a tree."

"How big is the tree?"

"You can't move it. It's a hundred years old."

"Okay. I want you to go home, but only if you feel safe there."

"Why wouldn't I feel safe?"

"Just a routine question."

"What, you think my old man's gonna pop me?"

"I didn't say that. Look, just get home before they miss you."

"What will you do?"

"I'll take care of everything."

"How?"

"I can't tell you."

Oberlin could not tell Billy Benigno how he would handle the situation because he wasn't sure himself. He pulled on his galoshes, grabbed his tweed overcoat and made his way across a sea of empty desks, and out the glass doors to the elevator. Benny C. was lying near death in the Benigno basement and Oberlin had to get to him tonight.

Billy had left the patio door unlocked. He managed to get back inside the house—before his father set the alarm for the evening—and climbed the stairs quietly, peeling off his jacket as he went, then ducking into his room.

"Billy! Dinner in ten minutes!" His mother's voice rang out from the bottom of the stairs, where he'd stood just moments ago. She was clueless, his mother. She hadn't noticed when he left, and she had no idea he'd just come home.

"Okay!" He called out. But first he needed to collect himself. He pulled back the duvet and got into bed fully clothed, exhausted not from the trip to the gas station, but from the secrecy, lies and treachery he knew he was inflicting on his father. He was a terrible son.

But at least he hadn't told Agent Oberlin about the blood. And maybe no one had been shot in the conference room. Maybe there was no dead body. Maybe his father's men were taking the rug to be cleaned because someone had spilled some blood on it. Some blood from a superficial cut.

14

Hayford Semple was eating soup out of a can with a plastic shoe horn when Oberlin let himself in. "We're going to Scarsdale."

"Can't you see I'm having my dinner?"

Oberlin grabbed the can and the shoehorn. "Finish it in the car."

Traffic was light on the Major Deegan Expressway. Oberlin got off at 161st Street and parked near the corner, under a streetlamp. He turned off the engine and cracked the windows to keep them from fogging over, and the two men scanned the shadows for Carmine R.

Semple said, "So, Victor just let him change sides? Just like that?"

"So far. And as long as he keeps his nose clean and provides some value to the Forte organization, he thinks he might have a future."

"In what."

"Just a future, period."

Hayford turned thoughtful. "Why is he agreeing to do this for you?"

"Five grand."

"Yours?"

"Yes, but I took it out of my vacation account, so I'll never miss it."

"What about procedure?"

Oberlin gave his partner a hopeless look. "That particular path is closed to me, Hay. I can't use legal means to enter the house because I got Benny in there illegally."

"You're pretty sure it's him in the tunnel?"

"Who else could it be?" Oberlin saw the look of despair on his partner's face, and interpreted it as compassion. "It'll be fine. It'll work out."

But Semple's attention was now drawn to the shadows, where—bent under the weight of a tattered rucksack—a short, stocky man appeared. Semple quickly raised his window.

"That's him!" Oberlin jumped out of the car and opened the back door for Carmine R., his load of explosives, and a suitcase-sized first aid kit. "All set?"

"Yeah."

Oberlin slammed the car door and got back behind the wheel. "This is my partner, Agent Semple," said Oberlin.

"How are you," said Carmine, glancing nervously out the window, and then at Semple's profile. "Have we met?"

"Briefly."

"Agent Semple was with me when we picked you up—"

"After D'Angelo dumped me. Yeah I remember." As Oberlin merged onto the northbound ramp of the Deegan, Carmine added, "I'm not happy about this."

Oberlin and Semple exchanged glances. "We don't expect you to be happy, Carmine. We just want to make sure this will work."

"Don't worry. When it comes to explosives, I know what I'm doing."

"What's in the bag, dynamite?"

"I never transport dynamite anymore. I use TOVEX, much more stable."

"And quiet, I presume?"

"No blast is quiet, but I've tinkered with it. Worst case it'll sound like a thunder clap, and not enough to wake up anyone at three a.m."

"That gives us thirty minutes," said Oberlin. "But we'll need more time to bring the bod—I mean, Benny—out."

"Piece of cake," murmured Carmine. He clutched the rucksack tightly in both hands, worrying the frayed handle like a strand of rosary beads. "I'm more worried about tomorrow. What happens to Carmine R.?"

Oberlin gulped audibly. "Look, if you want to pull out—"

"Never said that, Agent Oberlin. My word is my word."

"And five grand is five grand," said Semple, keeping his eyes on the road.

"Chump change, Agent Semple, when someone's life is at stake. I'd like to think this guy Cataldo would do the same for me."

"So, you'd do it for free?"

"Maybe. Doesn't make much difference. I don't expect to live past retirement—and then my wife gets everything anyway."

"Carmine knows I'll take care of him," said Oberlin.

"Yeah, sure," replied Carmine with a nervous snicker. "If there's enough left of me to ID at the morgue."

"No one can finger you for this."

"Are you kidding? This'll have my signature all over it."

"I can help you hide if it comes to that," said Oberlin with resolve.

They rode in silence for the next ten minutes, Semple with his eyes closed, an elbow propped against the window, and Oberlin glancing frequently in the rear view mirror to check on Carmine. Finally, he said, "Remember what I told you, Carmine. As soon as you detonate the explosive I want you to get away from the house. Go to the gas station at the Route 53 intersection. Someone will be there waiting to pick you up."

"How will I know who it is?"

"It's supposed to be really cold tonight, in the teens. My guy will keep his passenger side window open."

True to Carmine's promise, the blast was thunderclap loud, and just powerful enough to blow out the center of the tree and free the hatch cover, with little collateral damage. The two FBI agents stepped down into the crater and worked at the handle, which—due to its post-apocalyptic design—turned easily.

Semple hoisted the cover. Oberlin pulled it back and climbed in after his partner, taking three steps down the aluminum ladder onto the dark tunnel floor. Glancing up he saw a grim faced Carmine hesitating at the edge of the opening. Oberlin angrily waved him off, arms flapping like semaphore flags. He had every intention of seeing Carmine R. again. Alive, and in one piece.

Semple clicked on his flashlight. The men moved slowly through a small chamber that had been built as a bomb shelter at the start of the Cold War. The room narrowed to an opening the size of a sewer pipe, about five feet in diameter. They hunched down, knees bent, heads tucked into their shoulders. Oberlin tried to estimate their location in relation to the outside, but after about fifty paces he knew by the stench that they were closing in on Benny.

"Jeez," muttered Semple.

"No, it's okay," whispered Oberlin, his trained olfactory glands sensing every foul odor that could possibly emanate from a human body, except that of death. They were now at the end of the tunnel. Semple pointed the flashlight at the wall, then lowered it to the floor. There, leaning against the inside door, with a half dozen wine bottles between his stained pant legs, was Benny Cataldo, eyes wide open in a lunatic stare.

Oberlin reached down to feel for a pulse in his neck.

"Fuckin' took you so long," wheezed Benny, his cracked lips barely moving.

"It's okay, Benny," said Oberlin, getting down on his knees for a closer look at the sewer rat. "We'll get you out. But we have to stay quiet, and we have to move fast."

"Yeah? Just try keeping up with me, you prick." Benny's whisper was dry and shrill, like fingernails on a chalkboard. "I can't get out of this hell hole fast enough. Now get out of my way!"

Oberlin looked at Semple. They both took a step back, but Benny did not move.

"Alright, here we go," said Oberlin. He and Semple grabbed an arm apiece and hoisted Benny to his feet. "Can you stand on your own?" Oberlin's nose crinkled, and his eyes began to tear from the stench.

"Been standing on my own all my life, Oberlin. Why should now be any different?" Benny replied, then crumpled to the floor. They pulled him to his feet, and Semple hoisted him over his shoulder in a fireman's hold. "Let's just get out of here."

"Hey! My wine—"

"Shut the hell up, Benny."

Oberlin glanced at the wine bottles and the rifled cartons, and at a bucket, covered with a cement slab. "Benny, is that your..."

75

"Yeah, that's my commode. What about it? I'm supposed to crap and piss right on the ground where I sleep?"

Semple emitted a "Jeez," and Oberlin said, "Let's get him out, then I'll come back to dump this." He looked around, knowing it was the very least he could do, but realizing they had no time to do more.

When Victor sees this, he thought, heads will roll. And not necessarily guilty heads. He might blame Billy—the place was as messy as any high school party—and he wondered what Billy would say when confronted.

After hauling Benny out of the tunnel Oberlin returned for the bucket, then he pulled the hatch down, leaving the rest of Benny's mess where it lay.

Carmine R. crossed a deserted Route 53 and walked up to the dark service station just after three a.m. A solitary streetlamp cast a feeble light over the grounds, highlighting a pair of gas pumps and several cars parked neatly in front of the garage. Off to the side, pulled up near the restroom, was another car, dark and boxy. He moved toward it, making a wide arc until he came up behind it. The driver's side was in the shadow of the building. The passenger side window was down. He looked in, saw no driver, and hesitated. But Carmine was numb from the cold and spent from the stress. Using both hands to open the back door, he slipped inside and lay down in the fetal position to conserve warmth. *Oberlin's driver was taking a leak,* he reasoned. *Might as well stay out of sight until he gets back.*

A gust of wind whistled over his head, but Carmine R. was too exhausted to notice that the driver's side window was open as well. He had come to rest in a car scheduled for window repair in the morning.

Behind the garage, a glassy eyed FBI agent waited fifteen more minutes before raising his passenger side window and driving off.

15

Oberlin and Semple had left their car on an ice-covered trail in the dark woods bordering the Benigno cul de sac. They supported Benny as he walked, and when he stumbled they about-faced him for a better grip and hoisted him up by the shoulders. Benny's legs dangled in mid-air.

"I can walk!" he wheezed, and he pumped his legs furiously.

"No, you can't," replied Semple, at which remark Benny pumped even harder. "Keep that up and we'll leave you here for Victor and the boys."

All of Benny's leg pumping had caused a large wad of white paper to erupt from his back pocket and drop into the snow. "Hey, I need that!" Benny struggled and tried to pull loose, but the men strode on. Craning his neck to the side he caught Oberlin's eye and said in a choked voice, "Mark, please."

"What is it Benny?"

"Lemme just grab those, okay?" He pumped his legs gently. "It's no big deal to you. They're just some personal belongings."

As if on cue—and because Semple knew his friend so well—the men lowered Benny to the ground. As soon as his feet touched the snow he ran back ten yards, scooped up the wad of papers, and stuffed them into his pocket.

Semple shook his head. "And we've been carrying this guy? He should carry us." Semple moved on, followed by Benny with Oberlin close behind.

When they reached the trail, Benny sidled up to a white birch tree for a long piss. Oberlin left him with Semple and went quickly to the car. He pulled open the unlocked door, slipped into the driver's seat, started the engine and turned up the heat to maximum. He hadn't realized how cold he was until now. He pulled off his gloves and blew into his hands, and when the feeling returned he picked up his radio and called the agent responsible for meeting Carmine at the service station.

"I don't have him," came the short reply.

"Why? Where is he?"

"Never showed up. I waited fifteen more minutes, then left the scene." The voice was a crackle. "Want me to go back?"

Oberlin thought about this. "No. I'll take it from here."

He set down the radio just as Semple and Benny reached the car. Semple pulled out the first aid bag and set it on the roof, and Benny crawled inside, laying down across the seat. Semple closed the rear door and got into the passenger seat. "Problem?" he said to Oberlin, reading his features.

"I don't know." He backed the car carefully down the icy path from the woods and emerged onto a suburban street not far from the Benigno neighborhood. He thought about tracking down Carmine, but then he glanced in the rear view mirror and there was Benny, curled up in the back seat, shivering and muttering. Maybe he was delirious. They needed to get him to a hospital.

"Hang on, Benny," he said.

"YOU hang on," said Benny with a snort. "By the way I found the kid's bug in the conference room, under the table where no one would think to look. He did a good job. I'm a good teacher."

Oberlin and Semple exchanged a look. "So, whatever was discussed down there—"

"Could've been heard in any room with a speaker."

"Nice work," said Oberlin.

Benny said, "Don't mention it. And did you also know that Carmine's wife is screwin' around on him. Dumb fuck has no idea. Thinks it's all peachy with the little lady."

"Did you hear anything out of the ordinary while you were down there?"

"What? Hell, Mark. I was out of it."

"So, no gunshots?"

"Shots? No. So…someone was shot? Who'd they get?"

"No one. Just asking. Anyway, how do you know about Carmine's wife?" said Oberlin, keeping his eyes on the road.

"How do I know? C'mon, Oberlin. I'm the best in the business. I know he's being fucked over for his life insurance, which'll pay up after Victor finds him. Hell," continued Benny with a snort, "I also know that Schneider has a gambling problem…and that Pettini wore a wire. There's nothing I don't know."

At the mention of his informant, Pettini, Semple twisted around in his seat and covered Benny with a stony gaze. "Do you know where Pettini is?"

Benny laughed. "You're the one's supposed to be watching him, right?"

Oberlin gave Semple a quizzical look, but his partner turned around and settled back into the seat without another word.

White Plains had the closest emergency room, but Oberlin drove another ten miles to get Benny to a hospital that would not be on the Benigno Family's close-in radar, just in case they connected the backyard explosion to Carmine, instead of a fortuitous lightning strike. Oberlin dropped Benny and Semple at the entrance. He drove off to park in the lot and Semple, with one arm supporting Benny, reached into the pocket that held Benny's precious papers. Benny, nearly unconscious, offered no resistance, but a passing orderly stopped in front of them and gave Semple a menacing look.

"I'm not mugging him. Just helping to get him inside."

"I can see that. Lifting him up by the pocket."

"Ha. No, just making sure he has his insurance card. We're fine."

Oberlin joined them, nodded amiably at the orderly, and helped walk Benny into the hospital. There was no insurance card, nor any ID of any kind on Benny's person. Whenever he pulled a job, he liked to do so incognito.

"Do we check him in as a John Doe?" asked Semple.

"No, Benigno will be looking for a John Doe when he figures out what happened. Tell them we found him wandering along the road, and he said his name is Sam. Sam Richter." Then he said in Benny's ear, "Got that? You are Sam Richter."

Benny nodded. This was fine for him, just another hurdle for the Benigno Family if they came looking for him.

"I'm going to look for Carmine," said Oberlin.

Semple handed him the papers he'd lifted from Benny's pocket. "Take these. They might come in handy."

Oberlin glanced at the papers, then shot Semple a quizzical look.

"Just take them," said Semple, and he led Benny slowly up to the ER entrance. The glass doors parted, and they slipped inside.

Back in the car, Oberlin aimed his flashlight at the top page and saw the list of names and numbers, obviously evidence of a gambling racket, and he was about to stuff the documents into the glove compartment to await further scrutiny, when one name in particular caught his eye. Ken Schneider. *SAC Ken Schneider?*

So Schneider was doing business with the Families and this was the evidence that could ruin his life. This is what Benny knew, and would use if he got the chance. He'd also said that Carmine's wife was having an affair, and had just taken out a life insurance policy on her husband. It was part of Benny's M.O. to keep the affair quiet for a share of that life insurance payout. Which would only happen at Carmine's death.

Oberlin and Semple had saved the life of a double rat.

And at this moment Carmine's life was hanging in the balance. Oberlin drove out of the hospital parking lot and headed north toward the service station that was supposed to have been his valuable and cooperative informant's safe haven.

Oberlin drove slowly into the lot. The moon was full but the perimeter of the building was wrapped in a shadow cast by the fuel pumps. He lowered his window for a better view of the landscape. The air was bitterly cold and unnaturally still. The icy pavement crunched under the tires as Oberlin rolled slowly ahead, taking in the inert, unbroken outline of the setting. Three cars were parked in front of the closed bay doors, but parked cars at a service station, awaiting repair, were unremarkable. He drove past them, circled around to the other side of the station, and then returned to them. Something was wrong with this picture, and it took a moment for Oberlin to realize what that was.

The rear windows on two of the cars were clear. But the rear window of the third car was covered with frost, indicating a temperature difference outside and within. Oberlin stopped, got out of his car, and pulled his service revolver from his shoulder holster. The driver and passenger side windows were lowered halfway. There appeared to be no one inside the car, but he approached from behind, revolver poised in his right hand.

It was difficult to see through the shadows, and Oberlin had no light with him. He crouched down and crept up to the car below the level of the windows. There was no driver, no passenger, and nothing in the back seat except a blanket.

He was about to move on when he caught a glimpse of fur. It startled him, and he backed away, certain this was an animal sheltering from the cold. But the animal was still, and when Oberlin tapped on the car to provoke a response, none came. He opened the back door gingerly and looked down at not a blanket or a furry animal, but at the body of Carmine R. and his wild, matted hair. Poor bastard had been here all the time, in the wrong car, hunkered down for two hours in sub freezing temperatures.

But he was still alive. Carmine's breath, feeble though it was, had frosted the rear window of the car. Oberlin pulled his squad car alongside and transferred Carmine to the back seat. Now all Oberlin had to do was find an off-the-grid motel where he would bring Carmine back to life, while coming up with a long term plan to keep him that way.

Benny squinted at the bedside clock until the numbers made sense. It was three in the morning, and there were loud voices—daytime voices—outside his door.

"Come tomorrow at visiting hours," said a woman's voice.

"He's my cousin," replied the clear male voice. "I'm worried about him, is all."

"I'm calling security—"

"No, no! I get it. I'm leaving. I'll be back first thing."

"Not first thing!" said the woman. "Visiting hours start at 10 a.m."

Benny found himself clutching the edge of his hospital blanket, pulled it up to his chin and realized he was shaking. He had heard only one set of retreating footsteps.

A moment passed. There was a sound at the door, the metallic click of a doorknob, and he watched the shadow underneath, expecting it to widen, and his throat began to close. And then a click, and retreating footsteps, and Benny settled back into the bed.

He wanted sleep, needed sleep, but something nagged at him that he couldn't quite name. Name. That was it, the names. Where were his clothes with the pocket that held the papers with the important names, like Agent Schneider?

"I gotta get that list," said Benny.

"Are you talking to me?" came the voice of his roommate.

"Uh...no." Then, "Unless there's something you wanna tell me."

"What? Who are you?"

"No one. Never mind," replied Benny, figuring it never hurts to ask. "Just talkin' to myself. Sorry to disturb." He waited for the roommate to settle back to sleep, then Benny pulled out his IV, dressed quickly, and left the hospital in the dead of night.

16

There was no sign that Sandra B. had been disturbed by the sound of the blast. The heavy tapestry drapes were drawn in the master bedroom. Wrapped in a silk negligee, hair in curlers, she slept soundly under a thick duvet. Victor had said he'd be out for the evening, which was fast becoming the early morning.

The wind had picked up. A tree branch, stiff from the cold, rattled against Billy's bedroom window, and he awoke with a start. He slid his legs over the side of his bed and scanned the room, half asleep, *knowing* he was half asleep and vulnerable, and searched the dark instinctively for a break in the shadows. His eyes came to rest on his desk chair. Someone had left a pile of clothes on top of it, and he remembered the blood on the knees of his pants and wondered who had put the laundry right out there, on his chair, where anyone, like his father, could see it. He got out of bed and the mattress squeaked, and the pile of clothes sat up.

"What are you doing in my room, Clara!" said Billy, more startled than annoyed.

"That explosion scared me. Can I stay here for a while?"

"What explosion? That was a thunderclap!"

"There are no thunderstorms in the frozen winter, you dork!" Even in her fear, in a position of needing a favor, Billy's little sister could not resist a gotcha moment. "That WAS an explosion. And it was nearby."

"Yeah, well don't worry about it. You don't see mom freaking out, so it must be okay," said Billy, thinking it must be the Xanax. "Go back to bed."

"Can I just sit on the chair for a while? I promise I won't stare at you."

He was about to protest, but something in his sister's eyes told him

83

she was very frightened. How can you throw someone out of your room in the middle of the night if they're afraid of being alone. He went back to his bed, Clara went back to the chair. For a few minutes Billy listened to the frozen branch scratch against the side of the house. Then he pulled the top blanket from his bed, walked softly across the room to his sleeping sister and draped it across her shoulders.

The next day, Lisa Forte caught up with Billy on the high school steps. He'd seen her coming, but there was no escape through the tightly packed pods of students waiting for the bell. Moments later, her soft, lovely hand was on his shoulder. "Billy, wait. We need to talk."

He fixed what he hoped was a carefree smile on his face and turned around. "Sure! I'll catch you at lunch."

"Really?" She seemed uncertain at first, and then smiled, as if to bask in the affirmation of their relationship even though she knew at some basic level that this meeting would be their last. This would be the breakup lunch.

Billy's smile disappeared. "Actually, Lisa, I don't think it's a good idea to have lunch together."

"Today?"

He took a deep breath, and Lisa waited. "Actually…"

"You said that already."

"Oh, yeah. So, it looks like it's not a good idea for us to be together, because of the new setup with our families."

"They're working together. What could be better?"

"And also, my mother wants me to concentrate on school."

At the mention of his mother, Lisa's fake smile disappeared. "It's your mother, isn't it. Nothing to do with our families."

"Well, technically, she is my family…"

"Cut it out, Billy. Your mother tells you how to live your life and you listen to her!" Lisa felt the tears forming and blinked them away. "You should just grow up, Billy Benigno, and start thinking for yourself!"

The bell rang. Lisa ran down the steps to some girls who had been watching this exchange. Her posse, Billy thought. He hesitated, then shuffled inside with the rest of the student body.

Sandra answered the door still dressed in her negligee at nine that morning. She appeared to be mid-makeup, and the curlers had done their job, expanding her hair to gravity defying height and width. "What are you doing here?" She said, annoyed. "It's a school day." She looked quickly past Lisa Forte to see if her son was in the vicinity.

"No, Billy's not here," said Lisa with a touch of venom. "He doesn't know I came here, either."

Sandra squinted, trying to divine the reason for this visit, rather than subject herself to a lengthy explanation. "Look, Lisa. I know you're upset about this..."

"About what?" she said defiantly, even though she knew.

"You and Billy. It just won't work. He's too young to have a girlfriend."

Lisa took a couple of deep breaths to steady herself, then stepped closer to the doorway. "And you, Mrs. Benigno, are too old and sloppy looking to have a boyfriend!"

Sandra gasped. Her hand flew to her mouth.

"And in case you've forgotten, you're married! That's why your name is Mrs. Benigno!"

Sandra's highly arched brows rose further in disbelief. "What did you just say?"

"You heard me!"

"You...you think I'm old and sloppy?"

Lisa rolled her eyes and stepped back from the door. "My God! Didn't you hear what I said after that? I know you have a boyfriend!"

Before Lisa had time to react, Sandra reached out, grabbed her by the arm and yanked her into the house. "Now you just listen to me!" Sandra slammed the door shut and glared at the startled young woman. "I don't know what kind of drugs are causing your hallucinations, but I am a...

married woman," she said, avoiding the word *happily,* and I do not - I repeat, DO NOT - have a boyfriend on the side."

Lisa folded her arms defiantly. "Oh yeah? Well I think you're a liar."

Could this girl possibly know about Sandra's dalliance so many years ago with her father, Dante? Did her father confide in her, now that he was a widower, with no romantic companion? Suddenly light-headed, Sandra looked around for something to grab onto. Lisa stepped out of the way. "Oh my God. Never in my life…" She backed up to the staircase and lowered herself onto the second step. Now looking up at Lisa, she moved instead to the third step so that they were face to face. "Lisa, Lisa," she intoned, reaching for the girl's hand. "Who told you this ridiculous lie? Who told you I have a boyfriend?"

"No one told me. I saw it with my own eyes."

Sandra squinted. "You saw it? You saw what with your own eyes?"

Lisa let out a lungful of air. This woman was exhausting. "Okay, Mrs. Benigno. I saw you in the shoe department at Bloomingdales the other day. You were talking very…intimately to a guy with a beard."

Sandra was speechless for the moment.

"He whispered something to you, and then I saw you give him your keys."

"My keys?" Sandra glanced from side to side, stalling for time and searching for a plausible and innocent way to explain to this girl—the daughter of a well respected Mob capo—why she had given her house keys to an FBI agent.

Of course, there was none. Sandra Benigno was now involved with the FBI up to her cold-creamed neck. So she said, "Those were my car keys, Lisa! And…and the bearded man," now she was winging it, "was from the parking garage on 61st street. Yes, I forgot to leave my keys in the car and they needed to move it." She smiled at the finesse of her exculpatory statement. "See? Perfectly innocent."

Lisa blinked a few times. "So then, you pulled into the space yourself? They let you park the car?"

"I know!" She said with a snort. "Shows you how stupid they are!" Sandra continued quickly, before Lisa could protest, "But let's get back to the important issue. I'm trying to put some space between you and Billy for your own good as well as his."

"I'll worry about myself, thank you. Anyway, I don't believe you."

"About the bearded man?"

"About your motives—but yeah, that too."

"Listen, there are things I just can't tell you now, but some day you'll thank me for this." Sandra thought she saw tears forming in Lisa's big blue eyes. She was a very pretty girl, would probably become a beautiful woman, and why not? Her father, Dante Forte, was the handsomest man alive. Something tugged at Sandra B.'s heart. She felt sorry for Lisa, couldn't blame her for loving her son, and gave her points for her discerning choice of boyfriends.

She continued more gently, "I'm not doing this just for my son. It's for your sake too, Lisa. You just need to trust me on this."

"Is he in some kind of trouble?"

"Not yet. And I want to keep it that way."

These two—the woman and the girl—locked eyes. No more words were exchanged. Lisa's look said it all:

Sandra's secret rendezvous with the bearded man was safe, but only if Sandra stopped meddling in her son's love life. For now, Lisa Forte had the upper hand.

17

Clara was late for school. She'd missed the bus, and Sandra was still in her nightgown, still fixing her face with too much makeup, and in no mood to drive her. Something had annoyed her mother this morning. Clara hadn't seen Lisa drop by, so she assumed it had to do with her father. Her mother's misery always had something to do with him, at least that was what usually started her off.

Instead of the long walk along the main road, Clara decided to take the forbidden shortcut through the woods behind the house. No one would be the wiser. Her father wasn't home, hadn't come home at all last night, which was probably why her mother was in a sour mood, although she really never needed an actual reason.

Clara loved the woods in winter. The scenery was magical on this clear January morning, like a petrified forest, afraid that if it moved its branches and their few remaining leaves, they would crack like glass in the frosty air. Step after rhythmic step, she crunched the virgin snow, glancing behind every so often to admire her bootprints. At the tree line she came to a stop and gaped indignantly at the ground before her. The beautiful snow had been completely trampled. Large shoe prints, much larger than her own, broke the white expanse. "Hello?" She called out, but not too loudly. Clara knew that no one ever came to this out of the way woodland. Even in summer. There were ticks, poison oak, poison ivy— the parade of horribles her parents had impressed upon them since they were small. But this time of year, it really seemed strange to see signs of people.

She followed the tracks, somehow certain that no danger could possibly be lurking in this bright, shiny morning. And there, before her, were the blackened remains of the old tree that had been her father's nemesis since the storms in September. He'd complained about it, but refused to have the tree removers come and clear it out, for reasons she and Billy could not fathom. Nearby, the metallic glint of the hatch cover caught her eye. Finally free of the oak tree, she thought, and she wondered if her father even knew, and she hoped he didn't because it would be fun to give him the good news.

Clara surveyed the scene. She'd made fun of her brother for thinking it was a lightning strike, but according to her earth science teacher, lightning can happen even in winter when there are temperature differences in the upper atmosphere. Excited about bringing home this news, Clara pulled the hatch cover with all her strength, expecting it to be frozen in place. But it gave way easily, tossing her back into the snow. "What the...?"

Clara grabbed the handrails, then twisted around to face the ladder. She hesitated on the top rung. The handrail was slippery. She pulled off her ski gloves and threw them in the snow, then she grabbed the icy railing and looked down into the narrow shaft. I would be so great, she thought, to have a trusty little dog who she could take down there with her as a scout. But there was no dog. She was perched on the forbidden ladder all alone, but she knew that in spite of the unknown risks and the warnings from her father—or maybe even because of them—she, Clara Benigno, was going in.

There were eight rungs in all, and then she stepped onto the ground. A shaft of light illuminated only her immediate surroundings. The rest of the tunnel was black. Before stepping away from the entrance she reached into her backpack and pulled out a keychain with a whistle and a penlight, a Christmas stocking present from two weeks ago. She clicked it on and made her way slowly into the tunnel, shining the light on the floor as she went. She resisted the urge to make an echo with her voice, but she clucked softly, and was thrilled at the amplified clack that came back at her. The penlight lit her way forward, but to her left and right the narrow tunnel was black, and the edge of her boot sent a wine bottle scraping noisily along the concrete tunnel floor. Clara stopped in her tracks and aimed her light at the source of the commotion. She picked up the bottle and saw that there were more strewn along the passageway. She crept along further into the tunnel and came upon the crates crammed with books and papers looking as if someone had been in a rush to get out and tried to straighten things up, but not very convincingly. Clara felt butterflies in her stomach. She wrung her hands, trying to figure out what to do. Billy had been down here partying with his friends—maybe even with Lisa Forte. If their father found out there would be no end of trouble for Billy. He deserved it, sure. But last night her brother had been kind to her. He hadn't chased her out of his room.

Now, balancing the little penlight on one of the crates, she proceeded to collect the empty wine bottles and stuff them into her backpack. When that was full she took off her ski jacket and used the hood and the sleeves to stow the rest. Unlike the wine, the paper mess could be chalked up to mice, or rabbits, or raccoons. But she would dispose of these incriminating wine bottles right away, and save Billy's butt.

She put her arms through the straps of the heavy backpack, then climbed up the ladder, carefully balancing the bottle-laden jacket in her arms. She reset the hatch cover, then trudged out through the other side of the woods and quietly deposited the bottles in a neighbor's trash bin.

Clara put her ski jacket on and zipped it up to her neck, securing the hood tightly to her head. She was cold, and she walked quickly to school, eager to feel the dull warmth of her second period math class, and wondering how she would relate this discovery when she got home from school.

She wouldn't tell her father, of course, but she couldn't wait to tell her brother what she had found.

Clara crept into Billy's room and paused at the doorway. Her brother was hunched over his desk, working on something. Homework? She moved closer until she could see over his shoulder. The mechanical drawing set, in a shiny dark wooden box, was splayed open. This was one of Billy's Christmas presents, because their mother thought he would become an architect. Clara could not remember ever hearing Billy say he was interested in building. He'd never even played with blocks as a kid. Still, their mother liked the sound of what Billy could become: William Benigno, Architect.

Without warning, she felt a powerful oncoming sneeze. She put a finger under her nose and pressed, hard, but this was a towering tsunami of a sneeze, and it broke over her with a loud "Ha-choo!"

"Oh God! That's disgusting!" Billy wheeled around in his chair, protesting the mucosal droplets that rained down on his desk, dampening his work. "Can't you knock, Clara? I'm trying to do my math." Billy grabbed the paper, balled it up and threw it into his waste basket.

"Sorry!" wailed Clara, who truly was. "But you can save some of it!"

Before Billy was able to stop her, Clara reached into the waste basket, pulled out the crumpled paper, opened it up and smoothed it on his desk. "Uh-oh," she murmured. "Does mom know about this?"

"What?"

"That you're not doing your homework."

"I'm taking a break. Get out of my room, Clara!"

"Actually," she said, "That's pretty good."

"Think so?"

Clara nodded and they both admired the eight by ten tableau Billy had created, depicting a fleet of perfectly detailed US warships, firing at Soviet aircraft with commendable precision—thanks to a drafting compass, triangle and conical point mechanical pencil.

"Listen. I have to tell you something," said Clara. She sat on the edge of Billy's bed and looked at him somberly.

Billy smirked. "Mom and dad are getting a divorce."

"What?" Clara shook her head quickly. "No, nothing to do with them. It's about you." She inhaled deeply then said in a rush of words, "Dad's going to kill you if he finds out you've been partying in the tunnel!"

Billy was stunned speechless. So, Clara continued, "I was able to get in through the hatch because the tree is gone. I saw the mess, threw out all your wine bottles—"

"Wine?"

"Yes, wine!" she mimicked his feigned surprise. "Ha! You had us all fooled. When Uncle Enzo offered you wine at Christmas dinner, you made a face."

"Clara—"

"Wish they'd let me have wine. I'm almost twelve—"

"Clara!"

"Billy! I'm trying to tell you—"

"Please, just shut up, Clara," said Billy quietly. "I'm trying to tell *you* that I was never in the tunnel." He watched her process this statement and waited for a reaction. How much could he tell her, about his fooling around with the intercom and their father's business plans, about the blood on his knee and the sounds from the tunnel. About Agent Oberlin, and about Mr. Cataldo.

He could tell his sister none of these truths. So, he lied. "Look, it was a stupid party at the end of the summer," he said in a soft, humble voice. "Please, Clara. Don't tell dad, or mom."

"Don't tell us what?"

Billy and Clara had been so absorbed with this tunnel development that they never noticed Victor Benigno leaning against the doorway. How long had their father been there? How much had he heard?

Clara looked from Billy to her father, then blurted, "About the mechanical drawing set!"

"What about it?" said Victor. "I thought it was a good present. Your mother's idea, but I liked it anyway." Victor hunched his shoulders and gave a palms up request for further information. "So, what's the problem?"

Billy looked at his sister, who had suddenly clammed up. She was a good kid, couldn't rat out her brother even if their lives depended on it. "She saw me drawing this," said Billy, offering the crumpled page for his father's scrutiny. "I like to do war scenes."

Victor glanced at the paper, let out a loud laugh, then said sternly to Clara, "I don't want you snitching on each other. Understand?"

Clara nodded meekly, then shot a victorious grin at Billy.

Victor came into Billy's room and sat on the chair. "Listen to me, both of you. Some tree removal people are coming here tomorrow morning to clear out some of the mess back in the woods. You're not to go anywhere near the workers, or the tunnel hatch. Is that clear?"

"Sure," Clara said, a little quickly for Billy's taste. "Have you been in the tunnel, dad?" she asked innocently enough.

"I went down there to make sure the walls were okay. No damage. Just freak winter lightning." He grinned, and the kids knew he was about to try out a joke. "A stroke of luck! Haha, right?"

Billy picked up his war montage, eager to put an end to this paternal visit, but Clara was almost giddy with her secret knowledge. She decided to play the old man. "Dad, you know, it could have been an explosion."

Billy winced inwardly.

"So maybe you should call the police."

Billy's eyeball daggers flew straight for Clara's head, but she ducked and kept going. "Someone might have blown it up." She glanced at Billy. "Or maybe it was kids fooling around."

Victor Benigno rolled his eyes. That's just what he needed, more cops and G-men snooping around his property. "A rare electrical storm, Clara. They call this a phenomenon." With that, Victor left the room, closing the door behind him. *Kids,* he mused. *Always arguing about something.* But Victor remained focused on Carmine Rizzo. His explosives expert, formerly on the Benigno payroll, had transferred—with his blessing—to Forte. Dante was now reporting to Victor, but the Cappo di Tutti Cappi had no illusions of one big happy family. He intended to find Carmine and get to the bottom of this backyard explosion.

Victor was sprawled in the California king bed when Sandra entered the bedroom. This was an unusual occurrence in the Benigno household. On the rare nights that Victor stayed home, he didn't come to bed until Sandra was already pretending to be asleep, sometime after eleven. Sandra checked her watch. It was only nine o'clock.

He lay on his side like a bathing beauty, a little grin on his face.

93

"You okay?" she asked warily, refusing to acknowledge Victor's come-hither expression.

But he patted the mattress and growled, "Hey, come over here."

In terms of endearments, this was as close as Victor had come in almost a year to a sweet nothing. She stood frozen to the spot. On the one hand, a little nookie would be nice. On the other hand, Victor had been regularly getting his nookies with Miss Poland.

"It's been too long, Alessandra."

She winced inwardly. Victor used his wife's full name only during pre and post coital communications. She had to make a decision, and for that, she needed to buy some time.

"Gimme a minute, Vic." She went to the bathroom, shut the door and locked it, and stared at her face in the vanity mirror. There were lines, to be sure, but most of her skin was in its original place. She still had a jawline, below which her neck seemed to be holding its own. At fifty, she couldn't compete with Miss Poland. But if she were twenty-seven years old again, there would be no contest. That's why Victor had been hers all these years.

"Alessandra?" Victor queried from his perch on the bed. "Are you okay in there?"

He was worried about her. That was sweet. There were so many little things Victor said that she wanted to interpret as romantic, except for the fact that his words and his facial expressions did not frequently match up, like in a Japanese movie dubbed into English. You had to rely on your sense of what would logically come next. Movies tended to follow logic. With Victor, you just never really knew what he was thinking. Or, if he was thinking.

"Sandy! You almost done in there?"

JEEZ. "I'll be right out! Entertain yourself until I get there! Okay?"

She aimed a bottle of Eau de Givenchy at her neck...

"And don't squirt that shit all over yourself."

...then put it back down on the vanity. Victor was very sensitive to perfume, so she selected her most expensive moisturizer, with just a faint almond scent, and smoothed it quickly over her body, head to toe. To get things moving "down there" she thought about Dante as she turned off the bathroom light and went to Victor.

"What's that nice smell?" said Victor, snuggling up to Sandra's bosom. "Olive oil?"

"Yeah, Vic. It's olive oil."

When Sandra opened her eyes that morning she was face to face with her husband, who was snoring gently, the duvet pulled up to his chin. She realized she was smiling slightly when his eyes popped open. "Good morning," she said in a soft, gravel-tinged voice.

"Same to you. Sleep well?" he murmured.

"Umm. Really well."

"Good, so you can thank me later." Victor rolled over and added, "What's for breakfast?"

Sandra was speechless. Then she surprised herself, and Victor, and burst into tears, which soon became great wet sobs. She buried her face in her pillow, so as not to annoy her husband, but soon found herself cradled in his arms. He stroked her hair, and clumsily tried to dry her eyes with the edge of the sheet.

"I'm okay. I'm...okay, Vic." She sat up, smoothed her hair, and clasped her knees to her chest. "I must be stupid. I should be used to you and your remarks by now."

"Nah, it's not you, Sandy. I'm the jerk, and I'm sorry." When she said nothing to acknowledge this apology, he added, "Course, if we did this more often, I'd be better at the sweet talk."

She thought, *We don't do this more often because you're busy with Miss Poland.* But she said, "I'm over emotional. It's my time of the month."

"Really?"

"Really what, Victor?"

"You still get those?" Victor did not notice Sandra's slack jawed look of disbelief at his latest faux pas. He flung off the duvet and announced,

"I'm making breakfast, so you stay right here, nice and comfortable." He wrapped himself in a bathrobe and headed for the stairs.

Sandra pulled two armchairs from the corner of the room and set them up at the edge of the bed. Victor returned with an eclectic mix on a large tray—eggs, sausages, leftover pasta from the night before, blueberries still in their plastic container, and a large pot of espresso. He poured two cups and they sat together, sipping the strong brew.

"Vic, I gotta talk to you about something."

Victor assumed the subject would be Miss Poland. He took a deep breath. "So talk."

"It's about Billy."

At the sound of Billy's name, Victor's face turned red. "Again!? Can anything happen between us that doesn't include Billy? You're smothering the kid, Sandy! For Chrissake!"

"There! You see? Every time I mention him you go nuts!"

"Because you talk about him all the time!"

"You never do! Except to criticize him."

"What's that supposed to mean? Huh? When has he given me any reason to be proud of him? What's he done special?"

"You melt over Clara! What's she ever done special?"

Victor pulled in his chin and looked around his wife's face. "Are you a loon or something? What does this conversation have to do with Clara?"

"You have more patience with her, Victor!"

"Of course I do. She's a girl! Billy's a man and he needs to start acting like one."

Sandra took a breath. They glowered at each other from their bedside chairs. The subject was Billy, again, and Victor was on defense. He wanted to bolt before he said anything else that would set her off. She was needling him, and for what? Hadn't they had a good night together? What did the bitch want from him?

"Do you love him like a son, Vic?"

He was caught off guard sipping his espresso. He let it spill back into the tiny cup before replying to this latest insane question. "If he's my son,

I gotta love him! What are you doing this for, Sandy? You're driving me nuts!"

But Sandra heard nothing after the first part of her husband's remark. She said slowly, icily, "What do you mean, *if* he's your son?"

Victor screwed up his face, truly lost. "What?"

"You heard me, Victor."

"Yeah, I said if he's my son I gotta love him. So that must mean I love him." Victor gave her a funny look. "What do you think it means?"

Sandra picked up the tray and left the bedroom. Victor slammed the door.

18

The Pelican Motel, in a rural hamlet off Route 17, was a relic from the 1950's. Oberlin and some of his fellow agents had been coming here for years with informants, cooperating or otherwise. The owner, a slight man with wire framed eyeglasses, was Rich Dumbrowski, who'd retired years ago after some success on the Catskill comedy circuit. Nowadays, Rich had no discernible sense of humor, but he asked no questions and respected the privacy of all who entered his clean, spartan units.

But it had been two days since Mark Oberlin had checked into the Pelican with a man who'd looked like he needed medical help. Rich thought it best to check on them. He knocked gently. "Just the innkeeper out here. Are you gentlemen okay?"

The door opened slightly, and Oberlin's face poked out through the slit. "Oh, hey Rich. Yes, we're fine. Just getting ready to check out."

Rich peeked over Oberlin's shoulder to the bed, where Carmine sat, staring at a TV with an eighteen inch screen and rabbit ears. Rich pulled Oberlin outside and said quietly, "He doesn't look so good. I got a friend who's a vet."

"Can he get me a local doctor?"

"Who knows? But I'm sure he'd be willing to take a look at your friend."

"My friend is a human being, Rich." Oberlin studied Rich's expression, wondering if he was trying out a new joke.

Rich shrugged. "Just trying to be useful."

The innkeeper walked away and Oberlin called after him, "Thanks all the same, Rich. He's actually feeling better than he looks." Oberlin inhaled some of the clean, cold mountain air, then went back inside where Carmine was still gazing at the TV. Oberlin clicked it off.

"Hey. I was watching that," Carmine complained.

"No, you were just staring at it," said Oberlin patiently. "Listen, we've got to make some decisions about your future."

Carmine snorted. "What for? I have no future."

"Why do you say that, Carmine? Benny is in as much trouble as you are if Victor finds out about the explosion."

"Are you kiddin' me, Oberlin? I thought all you G-men were supposed to be smart and well educated."

"Well, we are, generally speaking."

"Then how could you be so stupid!"

"Hey, keep it down," warned Oberlin. He peeked out the window, then twisted the mini-blinds until the sunbeams disappeared from the little room. "There are several factors to consider. We need to assess the situation, make some decisions that will work."

"Work for you, you mean."

"Not just me, Carmine. Something that will work for everyone." Oberlin frowned. "I've never lied to you and I've never betrayed you. Have I?"

Carmine chuckled. "I guess time will tell." He got up from the bed and tucked in his shirttails. "Where's my jacket?"

Oberlin looked around the room. "I don't know. Maybe Hay has it."

"Semple? What's he doing with it?"

"If you'll recall, Carmine, we had to get you out of the woods pretty quickly."

"Oh, Jeez!" Carmine wrung his hands. "Maybe I left it there!"

Oberlin searched the room and quickly located Carmine's parka hanging on the bathroom door. "Here, you go," he said, tossing it to Carmine who hugged it gratefully.

"Thank God. If Victor had found this on his property—"

"Listen to me. The only way Victor could place you on his property is if Benny tells him. And Benny isn't going to do that, understand? Benny's working for the government. If he rats you out he's calling for mutually assured destruction."

99

"Okay, okay. So what's the next move."

"Regarding you?"

"Yes, regarding me! Who the hell else do you think I'm worried about!" He waited for a response from Oberlin, who was staring at the dark TV screen. "Mark? What's your solution to saving my butt? And look, I got no problem with the Witness Protection Program. You can do that for me, right?"

Oberlin seemed lost in thought, then said softly. "Unfortunately, there are certain channels—"

"We talkin' about me, or the friggin' TV?"

Oberlin faced the little informant squarely. "Please understand, Carmine, that qualifying for witness protection and relocation is not automatic. If I could arrange it myself, you know I would. But the fact is, it's up to the Justice department. They determine your eligibility, and to qualify, you have to be of significant value to them."

"Meaning..."

"As a witness, testifying for the government against the Benigno and Forte crime families."

"So? That's fine by me! I'll testify! Just hide me away somewhere until I need to appear in court. After that we can make it a permanent relocation and wipe out my past."

When Oberlin did not reply, Carmine continued, "C'mon, Mark. I know the FBI does this all the time, without going through the whole Witness Protection Program rigamarole."

"You've been reading too many books."

"Don't lie to me, Mark. Can you do it? Can you get your supervisor to approve it—based on my future value?"

The fact was, Oberlin probably could get Schneider to agree to some temporary housing arrangement, which would come out of the New York office budget. But as a practical matter, Carmine had not yet outlived his usefulness as an informant.

"I got other information for you, Mark!" Carmine continued, excitedly. "About Dante, and his kid."

"What kid?" Oberlin said quickly. "You mean Lisa Dante?"

"Lisa Dante, nee Elizabeth Mahoney," said Carmine, and Oberlin could tell that he was proud of this new information. And that he knew the word "nee."

"Nee," repeated Oberlin, just to make sure that Carmine fully grasped its meaning. "So her original name was Elizabeth Mahoney?"

Carmine nodded. "Dante and his wife adopted her when she was a baby. They got her from a Catholic orphanage.

"Where are the Mahoneys now?"

"Dead. She was an orphan."

Oberlin gave Camine an eyeroll. "If this is such a deep dark secret—"

"You wanna know, how do I know about it?" Carmine grinned. "It's my business to know these things."

The truth was, that as the proprietor of the most popular Italian bakery in the five boroughs, Carmine had long been privy to the personal chatter and gossip of its patrons, who came for the pastries—cannoli, tiramisu, svogliatelle, struffoli—after Sunday Mass, and ordered these in quantity for the entire roster of sacramental celebrations—baptisms, communions, confirmations, holy matrimony, and funerals.

"Does Lisa know she's adopted?"

"I'm sure she doesn't. And anyone who drops the penny on this— well, they got a death wish." Carmine saw Oberlin's expression change. "What's with you? Lots of people adopt, even Capo's."

Oberlin got up from the chair and grabbed his messenger bag. "I'm going to settle the bill. Then I'm going to drive you to the train station so you can get back home without an FBI escort."

"What? I'm not going home!"

"Listen, Carmine. The best thing for you right now is to resume your normal activities. If they see that you're back in the bakery, it'll seem like business as usual. Anyone who blew up Benigno's backyard would have to be crazy to come back to their old neighborhood." On the way out the door Oberlin added, "Oh, and Benny knows your wife is cheating on you and that she's taken out a large insurance policy on your life."

"How the hell does he know that?"

"He's Benny. He probably tapped your phone line." Then he added, "Tough luck about your wife, Carmine."

Carmine laughed. "I don't give a shit about that. And anyway, the joke's on her! I failed my life insurance physical." To Oberlin's look of surprise he added, "Yeah, that's right. I got chronic progressive kidney disease. No way they'll insure me for more than ten grand." He snorted. "Let's see how far that takes her and Mr. Big."

Oberlin added, "And Benny. He's got a piece of it too."

"How the hell did that happen?"

"He's bribing her to keep her boyfriend a secret."

"Really?" Carmine looked surprised. "Who from? I've known about Mr. Big for years."

"That's good. The less Benny knows about you the better."

Carmine grunted. "Big problem with Benny is—you never know what else he knows and who he's sharing it with. I'm tellin' you, he's a bad guy, Mark. Don't you even wonder," he asked, "how he knew about Pettini? And whether he took that to Victor?"

Oberlin gave Carmine a wry smile. "I think about it all the time."

Oberlin headed for the Metro North station in Tarrytown. Carmine sat in the passenger seat and complained for twenty miles, until Oberlin abruptly pulled off at a rest stop and ordered Carmine to go sit in the back if he was going to keep grumbling. Carmine continued to grumble from the back seat, only much louder, and by the time they arrived at the station Oberlin was more than glad to get rid of him. "Don't forget this stylish garment." He tossed Carmine's jacket to him through the window.

Carmine said, "Hey, I hope you know…"

Oberlin raised the window before he could hear the rest of Carmine's statement, but he assumed it to be… "what the fuck you're doin', Mark."

In thirty minutes Oberlin arrived at the hospital emergency entrance where he and Semple had brought Benny two nights ago. "I'm here to visit Sam Richter," he said to a young woman at the reception desk.

She checked a printed list. "Room 302. Elevator's down the hall to the right."

Oberlin rode up to the third floor. Room 302 was directly opposite the elevator. He knocked once on the partially closed door, then stepped inside. The bed near the door was empty and made up. No Benny. He went to the window-side bed and pulled open the privacy curtain. This, also, was not Benny.

An elderly man with oxygen tubes up his nose blinked a few times. "Do I know you?"

"Sorry, wrong patient," said Oberlin. "I was looking for Sam Richter."

"Can I help you?" A young nurse walked into the room and stood in the doorway.

"Yes," said Oberlin. "They must have given me the wrong information downstairs."

"Who are you looking for?"

"Sam Richter."

She looked at Oberlin for a moment. "Would you please step outside?"

"Excuse us," he said to the man with the oxygen tubes, then joined the nurse in the corridor.

"Are you a relative of Mr. Richter's?"

"No, just a close friend," said Oberlin. "Does it matter?"

"Not really."

"So? What happened to him?"

"That's what we'd like to know. He left sometime during the night."

"Doesn't the patient services desk get updates about these things?"

"Sometimes there's a bit of a lag."

"An entire day?"

"Look, there are trainees all over this place. They make mistakes!" She had lost patience with Oberlin, and her angry eyebrows took off like rockets. "And the fact remains, your friend is no longer here!"

Oberlin tried to wrap his head around this statement, even though there was no reason to ever assume that Benny Cataldo would do what he was supposed to do. "Anyone see him leave?"

"He might have been caught on a security camera, Mr..."

"Oberlin."

"Okay, Mr. Oberlin." She looked exhausted, and it was just the start of her shift. "Patients cannot be held against their will." She added, "He must have left shortly after a visitor came in."

"A visitor?"

"Yes. It was after eleven the night he was admitted. I told this young man to come back during normal visiting hours."

"Young? How young?"

"I don't know. Maybe he just looked young."

"But you're young," he said to the nurse, who looked to be just barely out of her teens. "So he must have been...what? Twenty or so?"

"All I can say is definitely under thirty. The lights were low. I didn't get a really good look at him."

"Okay. And did he come back yesterday?"

"I was off. But the floor nurse said that Mr. Richter's bed was empty and his clothes were gone when she did her 6 am rounds."

19

Ken Schneider crumpled up a piece of paper and sunk a rim shot into his waste basket from across the room.

"What's on your mind, Mark?" he said to Oberlin, who dodged the next shot and took a chair in front of Schneider's desk. "See all this paper?" Schneider pointed to the three tall piles on his desk, as if they were not self-evident. "I'm culling the wheat from the chaff because we don't have enough space to file it all."

"So what you're saying is that the scales of justice are influenced by our file storage capacity," Oberlin remarked, only half-joking.

"I never said that!" Schneider said, with a reflexive glance around his office for potential witnesses. "But I will welcome the day when we can all live paper-free."

"Speaking of papers." Oberlin handed Schneider a sealed legal envelope. "These might be of interest."

Schneider turned the unmarked envelope over in his hands. "What is this?"

When Oberlin did not reply, Schneider called his secretary on the intercom and told her they were not to be disturbed. One look at Oberlin told him he'd better open the envelope now. He tried a letter opener but could not find the battered seal.

"Let me." Oberlin pulled it from Schneider's shaky hand. He tore off the short edge, pulled out two sheets of notebook paper and handed them to Schneider.

"What's it about?" Schneider reached out, then pulled his hand away, as if the papers might burn him.

"I've already seen this, Ken. Do I need to read it to you?"

Schneider grabbed the papers from his hand. He took a hard look at Oberlin before reading them and setting them down on his desk. "I see you've highlighted the dirty parts."

"Your name appears in three places."

"Where did you get these?"

"Let's say I stumbled upon them out in the field." Oberlin watched his SAC's expression switch from challenging, to resigned. "Who's your bookie, Ken?"

Schneider sighed deeply. "WAS my bookie."

"Yeah, right. So who WAS he?"

"A guy named Palomino."

Oberlin laughed. "You're kidding, right? Palomino, like the horse breed?"

"Yes, just like the horse. Quite the crushing irony, isn't it?"

"Do you think there's any more evidence?"

"Yes, but only in Palomino's head. I think we can safely say that this—" Schneider pointed to the notebook pages"—is the extent of the physical evidence." He fixed Oberlin with a steady gaze. "I can take care of these, but what about your source?"

"I'll take care of my source. In fact, my source has made a rather small request that you have been unwilling to process."

"What the hell are you talking about?"

"The INS. Fast track to a green card for his relative."

Schneider thought about this. "That might be doable."

"And what about my operation?"

"You mean the Benigno *sting*?" He said sarcastically.

"D'Angelo and I are setting it up for Friday, noon."

"This Friday? You're crazy—-and *this* is extortion!"

"It's persuasion, Ken. And whatever you decide, we both know your secret is safe with me."

Schneider nodded. Oberlin was a man of his word—if not a man for rules and regulations.

"Ken, look at it this way. If Benigno pulls this off you'll never hear the end of it. The press will shine their high beams on SAC Kenneth

Schneider. I can see the headlines now: *Where was the FBI? Sleeping on the job? Or Playing the Odds?"*

"Okay, okay." Moments later a thought washed over Schneider's face. "So who is your source, Mark? Which one of your Benigno Squad TEI's has been whispering sweet nothings in your ear?"

"It might amuse you to note, Ken, that my TEI's are from the Forte family side, which—if you'll recall—I've been working for the past few years. I have no idea why you wanted me to head up Benigno—where I had *no* resources. It takes years to cultivate rats, Ken." He added wryly, "Or did you think they would just scurry into their new slots on your revised organizational charts?"

Schneider sighed deeply. Whatever course he chose now would present its own set of unintended consequences. "So that's it? You can't give me anything else—no solid piece of evidence—for sticking my neck out to support your little plan?"

"C'mon, Ken. If it weren't for—" he made finger quotes—"the Palomino Papers, you would have thrown me out of your office ten minutes ago." He watched uncomfortably as his boss saw his options, and maybe his future, slipping away. "There is one name," Oberlin finally said, "Sandra Benigno."

"Victor's wife? But how would she know? Wives are never privy to this stuff."

"She overheard the conversation on an intercom that was discovered by my TEI." He added, "In the lower level conference room."

"In their house?"

"Yes."

"Why don't we know about this conference room?"

"Same reason we didn't know about their underground bunker…"

"What?"

"…and the tunnel to the woods behind the house." He shrugged at Schneider's dropped jaw. "Why don't you ask D'Angelo why his Benigno rats haven't delivered."

"Okay, okay," Schneider brushed aside this not-so-subtle dig. "But why would she report her own husband…unless she has a death wish?"

"Ongoing marital hostilities. I won't go into all the personal details—"

"Good. So, D'Angelo is fully supportive?"

"Yes. And Agent Semple can back me up on all the details of Sandra B.'s story."

"Where is Semple? I haven't seen him today."

"No idea. But that should be the easy part of your job, keeping track of us."

"Yeah. Easy—like herding cats."

20

Oberlin phoned Semple from his desk. There was no answer, nor was there an answering machine, which was a breach of the unwritten OC squad protocol. Oberlin left the office without a word to the staff and walked the ten icy Manhattan streets to his partner's building. He buzzed twice and waited. Then he reached into his pocket and pulled out a set of keys, one of which was given to him by Semple, just in case.

Semple's apartment was on the third floor. Oberlin took the stairs slowly, automatically, pulling his service revolver from its shoulder holster, then pressed it to his side when a young woman with a large breed dog came running down the steps, almost smacking into him.

"Sorry!" She called cheerily as she and the dog careened down to the small first floor vestibule.

When he reached the third floor landing Oberlin stopped for a moment to gather his thoughts and plan his next moves. He had drawn his pistol as a precaution. But, against what? The facts were these: 1)Hayford Semple had not reported to the office all day, in spite of the fact that he had an excellent record for attendance and reliability; 2)Hayford Semple was working an OC squad with mob assassins and desperate informants who would do anything to achieve their goals of gathering wealth and power, while staying alive and out of prison; 3)Hayford Semple had a failed marriage and a history of depression, even though the clouds seemed to have been lifting, of late.

As a result of this assessment, Oberlin opened the door to Semple's apartment leading with his gun arm. He immediately saw his partner, seated on the sofa with his head drawn back in an unnatural pose. His service revolver lay on the floor. There was very little blood. The apartment was neat as a pin, a far cry from the mess it had been a few weeks ago. He studied the body of his partner. Special Agent Hayford Semple, who had never fired his gun in the line of duty, and who considered himself a pacifist, had shot himself in the head.

Oberlin felt his legs give out. He fell onto the sofa beside his partner's body, heedless of the forensic implications of his presence. He struggled to make sense of the scene. What had driven Hayford to this desperate act? What was the tipping point?

Then he saw it. Almost as if Semple had left them there to provide an easy explanation, two photos were propped on the coffee table. In one, he is smiling, arm in arm with Chaz Pettini, who'd been Semple's TEI before he disappeared. In the second photo, he's standing outside a bar with Pettini. The name of the establishment is hidden by a streetlamp.

Would he kill himself over the disappearance of an informant? No, thought Oberlin. Not unless they had been lovers.

That would mean that Semple had led a double life, and that Oberlin, his closest friend, had missed all the signs.

"You know, Mark, it's perfectly reasonable for you to take some time off. Maybe a day or two."

Oberlin walked back to the parking lot from the cemetery where Hayford Semple had been laid to rest. Until now he'd been able to avoid dealing with Semple's family, which consisted of an aunt who loved to talk about FBI work, and a surly step-son, Jonathan. Apparently, Semple's ex-wife chose to sit this one out.

Now Oberlin walked over to the step-son and waited while a young woman, roughly the same age as Jonathan, paid her respects. When she turned to leave, Oberlin stepped over to Jonathan and extended his hand.

"I'm very sorry for your loss," he said sincerely.

"Yeah. Probably more of a loss for you than me. This is the first time I've seen him in years."

Oberlin tried to read the emotion on Jonathan's face. There was no sarcasm, but certainly no show of bereavement. His expression and voice were flat and resigned. "Look, Jonathan. I know your dad was depressed, but I have no idea what put him over the edge." He reached into his pocket and pulled out the photos. "I found these in your dad's apartment. They were near him when he died."

"When he shot himself," Jonathan corrected him.

"If you prefer to put it that way."

"I don't prefer it," said Jonathan. "It just happens to BE that way. And I'll bet you think it was my mother's fault for leaving him, right?"

"Well, there are always two sides—"

"You're damn right there are!" Now Jonathan was shouting, and attracting the attention of the clergy as well as the mourners. Oberlin thought, *Okay Jonathan. That's enough venting for now.*

Jonathan took a couple of huffy breaths, then said with tears in his eyes, "My father liked men. There was no room in his life for my mother."

Oberlin found no reply. He looked at the ground while the young man composed himself.

"Sorry," he sniffed. "Don't know why I'm angry at you. He thought the world of you." Another sniff. "So you didn't know?"

"That he was gay? No. I thought he avoided women because he was still pining away for your mom." Oberlin glanced at the photos in Jonathan's hand. "So, the man with him, was more than just a friend?"

"How the hell would I know?" Jonathan glanced around, took note of the hallowed grounds, and lowered his voice. "Yes," he conceded. "I think so."

Oberlin offered the young man a few more meaningless words of condolence, then walked to the parking lot. A nauseating thought edged its way into his head. Benny had known that Pettini wore a wire. Had Benny bartered away Pettini's life in a deal with Victor Benigno?

Oberlin drove home like a hollow man, physically and emotionally drained. He rolled past the westbound exits on the Long Island Expressway, closing in on New York City and the game of cops and capos, and the human rats who play one against the other in an effort to survive.

But there was one rat who would lose this fight. Benny Benigno was a treacherous and compromised source who deserved to be exposed. Oberlin drove the rest of the way into town plotting, with grim determination, how he would cut Benny loose from federal protection, and hang him out to dry—without endangering other important informants, notably Carmine R.

21

Sandra B. drove her red Cadillac El Dorado into the parking lot of James Madison High. She jammed on the brakes, almost flinging Billy into the windshield.

"Mom! What the hell!"

"Why aren't you wearing your seatbelt!"

Billy grabbed his backpack and pushed the heavy door open with his foot. "You drive like a maniac, mom."

"Oh yeah! If you don't like it you can walk to school. Better yet, you can wake up on time and get the bus like all the other kids."

"Yeah, sure. I'll be driving soon, anyway."

Sandra put her hand on her son's arm, to stop him from exiting the car. "Sorry, Billy. I'm just a little edgy."

"No joke. So what's it this time?"

"Maybe I'm nervous about you driving."

"I'm taking driver's ed. They teach you everything."

"Really," she screwed up her eyes as she faced him down, and the fine lines grew like fissures in the feeble January morning light. "So tell me something, smart guy. What car are you gonna use?"

"Not sure. Maybe dad will get me one."

"Dad?"

"Yeah. Why not? I'll pay him back from my after school job."

Sandra's cackle sent Billy's left leg out the car door where it joined the other one for a quick escape. "What's so funny?"

"You don't have a job! That's what your father is always complaining about!"

"So? I'll get one." Billy ducked out the door and turned back to Sandra, who was expecting a "thanks, mom." But instead he said, "Dad thinks he might have some ideas for me." And before Sandra could locate her next thought, no less form a response, her son was loping across the lot to the school entrance.

She sat still, feeling her heartbeat, fast, but rhythmic. And she thought that was okay, being fast, as long as it wasn't skipping. But then the car started to shrink, she was sure of it. She blinked hard and the windshield came towards her like a camera lense moving in for a closeup. And the floorboard was moving, too, rising up under her feet, trapping her legs under the steering wheel, compressing her chest. And even though she knew this was not possible, the heat rose in her face and her lungs screamed for air.

Lisa Forte, another high school over-sleeper, gathered her things from the back of Dante's black Cadillac El Dorado. "Thanks, dad," she said into the passenger-side window.

"No problem. Try to wake up on time, okay?"

"Sure."

"And why haven't I seen Billy at the house?"

She shrugged.

"Don't you still need a math tutor?"

She shrugged. "Yeah, I do, but.."

"But what?"

"It's his mom. She doesn't think we should see each other anymore." Lisa walked off to class leaving Dante Forte to do a slow burn in the front seat. Sandra Benigno. Now she thinks her low-life son is too good for the Forte's. But before this perceived insult reached a full boil, the sound of a car horn pierced through Dante's genteel sensibilities. "What on earth—" He grabbed his keys and stepped out of the car, intent on locating the offending vehicle. The sound seemed to be coming from the end of the lot, and he followed it to the last car in a row of ten, a red Cadillac El Dorado. He knew before looking inside that he would see Sandra B. But he didn't expect to find her in this condition.

"Sandra!" He tried the door, then rapped on the window. "What are you doing? Open the door!"

What she was doing was leaning on the horn in a frozen state, and even when she smiled in recognition she seemed powerless to stop.

He ran around to the passenger side, yanked open the door and slid into the seat. He said, "Sandra, please," and pulled her hands gently from the steering wheel.

The horn stopped. They looked at each other. Dante pulled his hands away. "What happened?" he said gruffly.

"I don't know. Probably just a panic attack, but I'm okay now." Sandra tried to glance at herself in the rearview mirror. Here she was, sitting next to Dante Forte, and she was sure she did not look her best.

If she had been thinking out loud, Dante would have considered this an understatement. Her hair was partially teased, and partially collapsed where her head had lain on her pillow. Her eyes were lined and bloodshot. Dante winced inwardly, remembering that years ago Sandra had been a beauty. Ah, but in those days they were all beauties. Those were good days.

Dante straightened up and shot Sandra a severe look. "So what is this nonsense about Billy and Lisa not seeing each other anymore?"

Sandra gave a little self-conscious laugh. "Who told you that?"

"Lisa. Just now. Is it true?"

"Dante—"

"What do you have against my daughter? She's not as good in math and science as your son, but she more than makes up for it in the humanities."

"I never questioned her humanity," Sandra objected.

"I said *The* Humanities—language, literature…" Dante could see she was lost. "Never mind, Sandra. The point is, I don't appreciate anyone telling my daughter who she can and cannot associate with. I'll do that. I'm her father."

Sandra blurted, "I think you're Billy's father, too!"

The silence in the car was so thick that Sandra considered leaning on the horn, just to break through it. "Dante, I know this must come as a shock, but the timing is - was - perfect. Remember that night?"

Dante did not remember that night, but he began to think that

Sandra might be overstressed and delusional. Best to treat her gently. "I remember it...vaguely," he said.

"It was vivid for me, Dante."

"Er - yes. So you were saying? About Billy?"

"Don't you see it?" She pulled down the vanity mirror and aimed the visor at Dante's face. "He really does resemble you. Look at the eyes—"

"Mine are blue."

"Okay, so his are brown, but look at the shape."

Dante humored her and looked at his reflection. He wasn't quite sure how to handle this. He and his wife had adopted their daughter because he was unable to father a child. But in his world—the world of macho family ties—being sterile was as bad as being queer. He could not tell her that Lisa was adopted— because Lisa did not know this, nor did he ever want her to know. As he thought these things he felt his throat tighten at the implications for his already tenuous relationship with her husband, who had effectively castrated him. If he even knew they had had a fling there was no telling what barbaric thing Victor would do to him.

He needed a plan that would shut her up. And he came up with *Plan A*.

"Look, I'll take one of those paternity tests." He wouldn't, of course, but he'd get his doctor to vouch for him. His doctor owed him some insider investment returns a couple of years ago.

Sandra put her hand on his arm and clucked, "Oh, Dante. For a smart man, you can be so ignorant. Those tests aren't 100 percent accurate. Not even 60 percent. That's what I've heard."

Dante nodded. Sandra had certainly done her homework.

"So, you understand now why I don't want our kids together. They could be brother and sister."

Dante felt the blood rise in his face. "Did you say...anything to Lisa?"

"Of course not! I'm a mother! I'm sensitive to young people!"

"Did you ever stop to think," said Dante with forced calmness, "that this could be all your imagination?"

"No! And furthermore, I think Victor suspects Billy isn't his."

"What! Why?"

"The way he treats him. He's not loving like a father should be." She gave Dante a meaningful look. "There's an Oedipus thing goin' on in our family."

"But—Oedipus killed his father and married his mother. Different concept."

"Oh, I didn't know about that."

Dante sighed, "It's just a Greek tragedy."

"That would be pretty tragic for any ethnic group. So, when did this happen?"

"It didn't, Sandra. It's fiction." He let himself out of the car and walked around to Sandra's window. "So, please don't trouble yourself about the kids. And please don't say anything else to Lisa—"

"I won't."

"Do I have your word?"

"Of course, Dante."

He watched her drive away, and ignored her little good-bye wave. She had promised to leave Lisa out of this, but Dante couldn't trust the ravings of a madwoman.

He might need a *Plan B* to keep Sandra quiet, and for this, Dante was prepared to do just about anything.

22

On any given day, one or two low-life recruits who vandalized the city's parking meters for the Dante Family, would deposit their coin with Benny as soon as he opened up shop in the morning. Since he'd been away on his nefarious adventure for the past two days, a line of penny pilgrims had formed at his storefront. They toted messenger bags, backpacks, even women's shoulder bags, all bloated with at least two days of "take." To keep them honest, they worked in pairs, splitting fifteen percent of the night's haul and leaving the rest to Benny Cataldo—minus twenty-five percent for Dante.

This arrangement rankled Benny. Sure, It had been reasonable when he began the operation two years ago, but at this point, they should be paying him the lion's share of the take for operating a racket under the nose—and eyes—of the Feds. Oberlin knew what Benny was doing and allowed him to continue, as long as he maintained an air of legitimacy and professionalism. And as long as he remained Oberlin's informant and operative.

He had never let Oberlin down. He had even insisted, at the start, that his team pack their coin in small appliances, so as to seem like legitimate customers when they entered his shop. They came in with toaster ovens, blenders, electric percolators—any gadget that would hold five pounds or so of metal. One new guy arrived with a four slice toaster jammed with quarters and it took hours with a butter knife to dislodge them all. Benny finally put a stop to this phony appliance ruse when someone brought in a lamp with a brass base brimming with coins and left it on the counter. A legitimate customer came into the shop, and to test Benny's repairman skills, she plugged in the lamp and turned it on, almost frying them both in the process. Current and coin are a bad combination.

Sometimes the hauls were good, but you could never tell. If traffic was heavy and the city was crowded the mayor's meter jockeys would empty them several times a day. Worse, the NYPD was now aware of this little mob sideline, and even though none of Benny's crew had been caught in the act, he was waiting for the day when the hammer came down, and when one of his crew with a beef—and a death wish—fingered Benny as the pit boss.

Where would Oberlin be then?

It was a tough way to make a dishonest living, for sure. But Benny had the type of insurance that very few informants possessed. He counted his various "policies:"

1) He knew that Schneider was involved with a mob bookie, and when Benny called in his INS favor—something Schneider couldn't refuse—he'd be in for a big payday from his own Sicilian relatives.

2) He knew that Carmine's wife was cheating on him, which entitled him to a piece of Carmine's life insurance policy;

3) He'd helped Mark Oberlin break too many laws to mention, including Oberlin's tacit approval of Benny's coin racket, which netted him three hundred a week, on average.

Benny whistled as he tidied the long counter of his fix-it shop. He'd grown up thinking he was stupid, since he was regularly called stupid by his parents and his schoolmates, but Benny Cataldo was much smarter than he looked, and he had a steady job that required skills only Benny possessed. He was needed by the Families, and by the Feds, and this was a satisfying feeling indeed.

This self-evaluation made him question whether he was being adequately compensated. Sure, he was making ends meet, and he'd even managed to stash away about ten grand. But he wasn't really fulfilled. He had no romance, no one special in his life. Not because he didn't want a relationship, but because Benny Cataldo was queer. And Benny was resigned to spending the rest of his life in the closet, since the Families, all of them, had zero tolerance for *fanooks.*

"Hello, Benny." Mark Oberlin stood inside the doorway. Benny hadn't heard him come in, and Oberlin had caught him in mid-reverie. "Looks like you're feeling much better."

Benny stopped wiping the counter. He knew Oberlin would show up sooner or later, but he wasn't prepared to switch gears. He bought himself some seconds while elaborately folding the dirty rag and stowing it neatly in a corner.

"Yeah," he finally replied, amiably. "What can I say? I got a business to run here."

"For now," said Oberlin. He took a few steps to the back of the shop and settled onto a wooden folding chair. "Know where I was yesterday afternoon?"

"Ha. Hope you weren't at the hospital looking for me. I felt fine. Checked out early."

"Sort of like Chaz Pettini."

"What?"

"He was thirty-two."

Benny stared at Oberlin. "What happened to him?"

"So you knew him," said Oberlin evenly.

"Look, why do you keep talking about him in the past tense? He's a Forte soldier."

Oberlin waited for more.

"Did he go missing or something?" Benny grabbed the dirty cloth and started wiping the counter all over again. "Yeah, too bad about Chaz. So," he continued quickly, "You were saying?"

"I was at the funeral, Benny. I met his son."

"Huh," Benny grunted, "That's gotta be tough on a kid, especially a son."

"Did you know Chaz was gay?" said Oberlin, who couldn't bring himself to use the mob vernacular, and yet doubted that Benny would understand the word queer. "Benny," he repeated when he got no answer. "Did you hear the question?"

Benny C. put down the cloth and turned to face Oberlin. There was something very close to dignity in his voice as he said, "Of course I knew. We can spot each other a mile away."

This time it was Oberlin who needed a moment.

"That's right, Mark. Your dumb, low-life informant is also fanook."

"Hey, that's your personal business," Oberlin replied coolly. "That should have been Pettini's own business too."

"What?" Benny smiled incredulously. "You think Victor had it in for him because of that? C'mon, Mark. This is 1980. Anyway, why whack a valuable soldier for that when there are so many better reasons to do it?"

"Like wearing a wire for Agent Semple?" offered Oberlin.

"Well, yeah. I think that would qualify."

"So, tell me Benny. You knew Pettini was wearing a wire. How can I be sure you didn't play this one?"

"I guess," Benny said with a shrug, "You'll just have to take my word for it."

Oberlin got up and moved slowly towards the door. "I can't, Benny."

"That's your problem, Mark."

Oberlin eyed him for a moment. "I don't think you understand. There's nothing left for you. I gave Schneider the notebook pages."

Benny smiled slowly. "Ha. So that's where they went."

"Yes. So, Schneider's off the hook. And as far as Carmine goes...well, I suggest you pay him a visit at the bakery. Buy a few cannoli and some tiramisu. Throw yourself a party."

"But—what about the tunnel? What do I get for that?"

"What do you get?" Oberlin swept his arm around the shop. "You get this, for the time being. And anyway, what good did you do in the tunnel? All you did was confirm what I knew about a live intercom feed. D'Angelo is heading up the joint OC squad now. I have my own problems."

Benny's laughed, carefully, so that it sounded more like a snort. "We're all victims of new management, Mark," he said, referring to the hostile takeover of the Forte Family. "In the meantime, while all you guys are playing musical chairs and comparing the size of your dicks, it's the little guys like me doin' all the heavy lifting."

"You're not an indentured servant, Benny," replied Oberlin, thinking that was precisely what an informant was.

Benny watched Oberlin walk out the door just as one of his meter jockeys walked past him into the shop. The disheveled man smelled like booze. He toted a heavy canvas pack on his shoulder. "Where do you want it?" he said.

"Drop it there." Benny pointed to a clear spot on the counter. The scruffy man set the bag down and shuffled impatiently. "We gonna do this now? 'Cause I got an appointment—"

"You got shit!" Benny shouted. He needed to clear his head and deal with a new situation. There were always new situations. Just when you thought everything was under control, something came along to spoil it. There was never a solid moment to enjoy what you had worked for, to just *be*. He was living non-stop, from minute to minute. There could be no *now* for him to *be* in. He was too busy assessing everything coming at him from the future. And this was the way he would live his life, if he intended to keep on living.

He hadn't given the Feds anything decent in a couple of weeks, and Benny could feel his power waning, like he was superman, and the bag on the counter was filled with kryptonite, instead of coin.

He pinched his eyes shut and said quietly to the man, "Just gimme a minute, will ya?"

Sounded like Oberlin was cutting him loose. Sounded and felt like it. Need something on... someone. Carmine, that's it. Rat out Carmine for blowing up the Benigno bunker.

No, you stupid shit. What good would that do? Carmine would rat you out for being in the bunker in the first place. Anyway, Victor already knew it was Carmine, he'd be an idiot not to figure that one out.

Victor was no idiot.

A dangerous game you've been playing, Benny my boy. Who was it that said, 'It's alright to rat, but you can't re-rat.'?

But then a thought came to Benny. It started as a flickering image in his brain, and as he ran it fast it gained substance... a woman... a woman with a perpetual scowl... a dumpy woman with a perpetual scowl... and tiny feet. A dumpy woman with a perpetual scowl and tiny feet...with a life insurance policy in her hand.

More likely than not, Carmine's life was now nearing its end. Time to hit up Lorena for a bigger slice of her husband's life insurance pie.

23

Carmine's bakery was on Arthur avenue in the Belmont section of the Bronx. Back in the day, Prohibition had been the big organized crime moneymaker in this neighborhood. Now, Arthur Avenue was a quietly suburban enclave of the Italian American dream. There was very little crime because the Families took care of each other, with their own brand of criminal activity, and justice.

Typically, the bread and pastries were baked in the early morning. The aroma would drift out onto the street, enticing passersby, and on weekend mornings, soothe the nerves of local customers—many of them armed—who had to wait in line.

Benny walked into the shop with a big genial smile on his face and extended a hand to his pyrotechnic savior. "Hey Carmine!" he approached the explosives expert who took his hand in his own doughy one.

"How ya doing' Benny? Okay?" He peered closely at Benny's face. "You look none the worse for wear."

"Yeah," Benny glanced around the empty shop, but asked anyway, "We alone?"

"Yeah, sure!" Carmine heard the door to the back office open and close. "Lorena's here too. But that's okay."

"Is it?" replied Benny, raising a brow. And then Lorena stood in front of him, all five foot two, three hundred pounds of her. "Uh, hi, Lorena. How's Trix?"

"What the fuck are you talking about?" replied Lorena, throwing a hostile glance at her husband. "What's he doing here?"

"Uh, I don't exactly know."

"Why don't you ask him? Never mind, I'll ask him." She leaned toward Benny. "Okay, so what *do* you want?"

Benny's smile was stifled by her menacing glare. "Whaddya mean, what do I want? Just came to give you my regards."

Eyes narrow with suspicion, Lorena looked from one to the other. Then she said, "Carmine and I are back together." She shot Carmine a dagger. "Aren't we Carmy?"

Carmine shrugged, then took a look at his wife and added quickly, "Yes. We're happily back together."

Lorena threw Benny a stiff smile. "So I guess you got no business here."

She turned on her tiny feet and went back to her office. She poked her head out the door to add, "There's a half decent bakery three blocks away. I suggest you go there for all your future bread and pastry needs."

Lorena left the shop at six o'clock. Carmine held the door, then pulled it shut and turned the sign around to *Sorry, We Are Closed.* After the din of the customers all day long, the empty, silent shop was soothing. He busied himself with the sales receipts, deciding that the day had been a good one. Delicately, he picked over the remaining baked goods destined for the Good Will bin, and selected a particularly plump cream puff which deserved a better fate. He popped this into his mouth and eyeballed several others as he chewed contentedly. Sampling the wares was something Carmine tried hard to avoid. The same could not be said of his wife, and poor Lorena had ballooned from a size six to a fourteen over the years. *Ah well. Hazards of the trade,* Carmine thought, noting that he never really liked his wife, even when she was skinny.

In fact, as he was about to sample a stray cannoli, several other hazards of the trade stood in front of the shop, one of whom, Victor Benigno, beckoned to Carmine with his finger. Carmine jumped to his feet, tossed the cannoli back into the leftover bin and hurried over to the door. He unlocked and held it for Victor. "Good to see you, Mr. Benigno!" He felt the dots of sweat prickle his forehead. He knew his voice was too bright, but he was afraid it might crack due to nerves, so he turned up the volume. "Come right in. What can I get you? Espresso? Cappucino? Spumoni?" He felt himself grinning like an idiot. "Please, have a seat!" Carmine made an expansive gesture to include the two soldiers, but they demurred, each with an unpleasant smirk, and waited outside. One of them was a former Forte soldier, reminding Carmine how quickly loyalties can change and empires crumble.

"So, my friend," Victor began in his curious stilted English that was neither accented Italian nor New York dialect, but rather a phenomenon Carmine thought of as *old neighborhood capo* speech. No one else spoke that way, which is probably why the powerful old capos did. Victor continued, "Maybe you have heard about the explosion in the woods behind my house?"

Carmine hoped his flushing face wasn't too noticeable. Of course he was expected to know about it. Until his recent—and pointless, as it turned out— switch to Dante Forte's side, he had been a rat for Victor. Carmine was supposed to know everything. But what was the correct answer for this particular moment? Why was Victor even asking him? And why come here with two soldiers to ask it?

"I did hear something about that. Thought it was a lightning strike," replied Carmine, palms up and shoulders raised, as in *you gonna tell me different?*

"Bullshit," barked Victor. His eyes remained hard on Carmine until the little baker was forced to drop his gaze.

Carmine felt the sweat run down his back. *He knows it was me. He'd be crazy not to know. He's here to kill me. He's going to leave and his goons are going to kill me, right now. I'm nothing to him, not even a speck of dust. But...why would he bother to come here at all?* This latest thought brought Carmine back from the land of the not yet-deceased. Hope sprang.

"Is it? Bullshit, I mean?" Carmine said, thankful he was able to speak.

"That is what I need you for," said Victor with a hint of a smile. "You know I value your professionalism and your discretion..."

"Thank you..."

"And of course I never would have known about Chaz Pettini if you had not provided me with that particularly significant information…"

"Look, Mr. Benigno, I only knew about his…personal preferences from a third party—"

"I'm not referring to his homosexuality," said Victor in a bored tone. "Why do I give a shit about that?"

"Oh, about the wire," said Carmine with a nervous laugh. "Hey, that was— *is*— my job, right Mr. Benigno?"

"Yes. And speaking of jobs, I have another important one for you. I want you to go out into the woods behind my house, tonight at midnight sharp, and tell me what you think about the explosion. You told me that every explosion carries the fingerprints—and sometimes the fingers, haha—of the person who set it."

"I…did say that, yes."

"Okay, so do some expert investigating for me and tell me what you find."

"Of course, Mr. Benigno, but—at midnight? In the dark?"

"I am sure you will agree that this must be done under cover of darkness. We do not want to involve the Feds. They are all over my operations as it is, right, Carmine?"

Victor's cryptic delivery, coupled with his tendancy to avoid contractions, was disorienting. Carmine's brain reeled at the implications, but he heard himself reply, "Whatever you say, Mr. Benigno."

"Good. So I will expect you to be in the woods behind my house at midnight." He added with a serpentine smile, "You can bring your own light."

"Uh, yeah. Sure." Carmine replied mechanically. Then he added in a voice full of hope, "And I can give you my report first thing in the morning. Okay, Mr. Benigno?"

"Report?" said Victor, and Carmine thought he noticed the Capo's face go hard, but Victor replied genially, "Yes, of course. But I might get a late start tomorrow morning, with all the snow. So don't kill yourself over it."

Victor Benigno ended the meeting abruptly and strode through the shop. A Benigno soldier opened the door for the Capo, then shut it with a bang.

Silence filled the room. Carmine sat stiffly in his little chair. He paraphrased Mark Oberlin in his head: *"Victor would never expect the person who blew up his backyard to come back to the old neighborhood." Maybe this was true. But maybe Oberlin was setting him up.*

He got up and moved slowly to the espresso machine, fussing with the buttons as if he'd never used it before. He finally brewed a cup, brought it back to his chair and sat down heavily. He sipped the steamy thick brew, his eyes tracking the second hand sweep of the wall clock.

Even though Carmine Rizzo was fairly certain that this would be his last night on earth, he felt oddly calm. He didn't want to die, but he needed a break from this life. He'd been skating on the edge of an abyss for years now, with nothing to show for his work, no real achievement apart from remaining alive.

Carmine knew he was living on borrowed time. This was the life of a Mob Rat. He'd informed on his Family to the Feds, and he informed the Family of the latest threats to their security by other Family members, as well as the Feds. All of which required cunning, opportunity, as well as a sizable set of balls, especially when trying to keep all sides from figuring out where the leaks were coming from. It also called for constant deflection—pointing to another wiseguy, whether family, friend or foe, as the source of a leak before it could be traced back to him.

Mostly, though, survival for a Mob Rat depended on dumb luck.

He glanced around the shop. He would miss his beloved bakery, but he'd expected to lose it anyway, as it was operating at a loss, and the creditors were closing in. On the bright side, even though he'd always kept the business end of the bakery away from his wife's prying eyes, she'd soon have to deal with this shit all by herself.

Carmine sighed. He'd be getting a break from it all. He would have preferred a less permanent one, but peace has its price.

Lorena Rizzo arrived late at the bakery. She flicked on the lights and scanned the place for signs of life. Camine hadn't come home for dinner and hadn't let her know, which was not unusual, except this time they had made a pact to try and save the marriage. Her idea, not his, and only because her boyfriend had bolted, and it's never good to be without a partner. It's not respectable. And so she had decided to go back to Carmine.

She pushed through the door to the kitchen and noted with satisfaction that it was neat and clean, just as she had left it hours ago.

But there was no Carmine.

She checked the lavatory. It hadn't been used, the toilet was spotless and the sink clean and dry. No Carmine.

"Carmy?" She called, feeling a catch in her voice. "You here?"

No answer. She moved slowly towards the basement stairs and peered down into the gloom. Then, Lorena being Lorena, she plodded heavily down the steps, pausing midway to scan the scene.

"Carmy?"

Cardboard boxes and bags of flour were stacked high in the little space.

"Carm?" She held her breath. There was no sound of life.

But there, poking out from behind a tower of boxes, was a bright yellow stain on the cement floor. She barged toward the boxes and rounded the corner. "Carmine!?"

A yellow rain slicker lay in a heap. On top of the slicker lay the top flap of a carton, with a message scrawled in magic marker:

Lorena, I'm not dead and I want to keep it that way. But when I am dead they'll probably never find my body. So maybe you should stop paying the premiums on that life insurance policy.

There was a P.S: *And take this yellow piece of shit back to Macy's for a refund.*

24

Midnight in the Benigno backyard.

With his car parked at the train station a mile away, Carmine hikes up a hill to the Benigno cul de sac in the empty, eerie black of night.

The suburban house, fifty yards from the road, is lit up like an amusement park—or a prison—and Carmine heads for the shadow of the woods behind the house. Away from the lights of the Benigno mansion, the snow is disorienting. Carmine gauges the likely distance of the tunnel from the back of the house and stakes out a spot on the perimeter. From there he makes two forays deeper into the woods, before his third attempt brings him to the blast field, which is now a glistening blanket of snow. There are no tracks—neither animal, man made, nor made man.

The shaft of the bunker tunnel is a large black hole surrounded by white powder. A frosted doughnut. He takes out his penlight, then tucks it back into his pocket. It is a futile and deadly assignment. Any evidence he finds will point to him. Unless he can find something belonging to Benny, something Oberlin and Semple dragged out of the tunnel when they hauled Benny out. He feels a spark of hope, but it fails to ignite as he imagines his exchange with Victor.

"So, you believe it was Benny who blew everything up?"

"Yes. Who else could it be?"

"You, Carmine. It could have been you. But I'll tell you what, let's pay Benny a visit and see what he has to say on the subject."

He pushes the fear away, but it comes back at him, flushing his face in the icy night air and sending streams of cold sweat down his back. He looks around for a weapon, and a barrier—a tree thick enough to provide cover. Where will they come from, and how will they kill him?

Carmine moves towards the bunker shaft, and aims his penlight into the abyss. If the fall doesn't kill him, it will cripple him. And he would cry out, and then they would find him and finish the job.

Carmine doesn't hear the soft *fwut-fwut* of footsteps in the snow. But the frosty exhale of heavy breathing slips into his peripheral vision. He changes his grip on the penlight, to weaponize it, with the tip protruding from his fist, but then the yellow glow skitters along the snow, creating a lighted path to where he now stands.

"A penlight? Seriously?"

Carmine turns and locks eyeballs with Benny Cataldo. "What are you doing here?" He feels his back stiffen. He needs to calculate his chances, but can't move his eyes from Benny to see if he came alone.

"Freezing my ass off," Benny says, digging his hands into his pockets.

"Victor sent you to take care of me." He takes a step back.

"Yeah. But that's not gonna happen, Carmine." Benny takes a step forward.

Carmine turns to run, but trips on a buried tree root, and from an undignified position flat on his butt, he looks up and says with a plaintive wheeze, "I saved your life, Benny!"

"Calm down, and lower your voice. No one's dyin' tonight, Carmine."

"Do you mean that?" Carmine picks himself up, eyes still locked on Benny.

"If I wanted to kill you, you'd be dead already."

"How?"

"What?"

"How were you going to do it?"

"I just told you, you dumb fuck, I didn't come here to kill you."

"Victor thinks you did."

"Let Victor think what he wants."

But Carmine is not reassured. His breaths came quickly, like little wisps of cotton in the icy air. He staggers backwards.

"Oh Jeez, Carmine. Are you having a panic attack? Because now is not the time."

Carmine's eyes turn saucer-sized.

"Okay, look," says Benny, trying for a soothing tone. "If I had wanted to kill you I would have just pushed you down the shaft over there. You were standing on the edge."

Carmine's breathing slows. "Yeah, but that might not have killed me."

"Okay, so I throw a few big tree limbs down on top of you to finish you off."

Carmine ponders Benny's logic. "Maybe, or maybe they just graze me."

"Jeez, Carmine!"

"Okay, okay. So why *are* you here?"

"I told you. I was sent to take care of you."

"And what? Lost your nerve? Or maybe lost your gun? Pretty gutsy to be out here without a weapon."

"Yeah? And what about you, coming out here in the dead of night, in the Capo's backyard, with just a penlight." Benny shrugs, "Anyway, Victor said to improvise— no noise, no bullet casings, no evidence for the Feds. But let's stop the jabber, I got a business proposition for you." Benny takes a deep breath and lets out a long stream of vapor. "We gotta face the truth. We're both dead men walking —you, for sure, since I've been sent here to kill you, and me…well, let's just say I'm being squeezed out of the new organization. Victor'll hit all Dante's guys, one by one, eventually. It's just the nature of the beast. He can't trust us, and he can't trust any of us who defected to Dante," he adds with a nod at Carmine. "We got a lot in common, Carmine. Both working for Oberlin…"

"I *worked* for Oberlin, Benny. Past tense. He knows I'm getting out, and he's gonna help me."

"Yeah, sure."

"No. He's solid. I've done a lot for him."

"Yeah, but does he know *everything* you've done?"

"What are you talking about?"

Benny shrugs. "Maybe I'm talking about Pettini."

"What about him? That was your move."

"I didn't give him up," Carmine.

132

"Oberlin thinks you did."

"Yeah, but we both know it was you, Don't we?" He waits a tick. "But maybe Oberlin won't believe me if I tell him it was you. The guy hates me." When Carmine makes no attempt to dispute this, Benny adds, "Or, maybe he's through with both of us."

Carmine shakes his head, "I got too much on Oberlin. He broke all kinds of laws. He let *me* break laws on his watch."

"Yeah, but here's how it works, Carmine. Oberlin *is* the law. And we're just the garbage rats."

They stare at each other in silence, then Camine says, "Okay. So what's your plan?"

Benny extends his hands, palms up, as if about to say the most obvious thing in the world. "We go with the Russians."

"The Russians?" Carmine screws up his eyes and peers into Benny's face. "You serious? What would they want with a couple of rats like us—"

"They want what we know, Carmine. That's how this game works."

"Ok, so we give them what we know about Victor, and his plans for the auto job—"

"And what the feds are planning. So, we basically save their franchise."

Carmine is pensive. "I'm not sure you've thought this through, Benny. Like what happens after we give them what we have and they don't need us anymore?"

"Simple, we just have to make ourselves indispensible."

"How? We gotta disappear ourselves from Victor and the old scene. If we're out of the loop, we won't know what they're planning. We got nothing."

"But we still have the Fed connection."

"You crazy, Benny? Weren't we just saying how Oberlin would just as soon see us dead?"

"Things change. We can be very useful to Oberlin through our new association with the Russians."

"Did he tell you that?"

"No, he doesn't even know it yet. But if you're in, I'll have deals for the Russians and the Feds by tomorrow."

"I gotta think."

"There's no time to think. Are you in?" Benny slowly pulls his hand from the pocket of his parka—and Camine dives behind a nearby tree stump. "Oh, Jeez. It's just my hand, Carmine. To seal the deal."

"Oh, yeah. Sure." Carmine gets up and brushes himself off. "Just... still a little jumpy." He accepts Benny's hand for a single, determined shake.

"We gotta trust each other, Carmine."

"Yeah."

"Like I said, nobody dies here tonight."

The new partners plod through the snow to the end of the woods, giving a wide berth to the Benigno property and its piercing lights. They find themselves at the entrance to the cul de sac at the bottom of a hill. They walk right past the two men who emerge from the Benigno property fifty yards away. They are young men, twitchy with adreneline, but they hesitate, confused by what they now see.

"There's two of them," one whispers.

"No shit," his partner replies.

Victor had calculated that Benny would finish off Carmine, and then come to a tragic end on his way home. He sent these two young wiseguys, who were eager to make their first hit, not anticipating a glitch in this plan.

They are not dressed for the cold, and they jam their hands into their coat pockets. "We got one bat," says one, pressing it to his side to keep it from slipping out from under his arm. "One rat, one bat. So what do we do now?"

"Okay, look. We still have the element of surprise."

"Yeah, and still one bat."

They pick their way gingerly through the snow, following the moving figures up ahead. Words pass between them in the wisps of vapor that hover in the still night air, as they plot their line of attack, while protecting their fine leather shoes. They'd had shoes-shines earlier that day, by the guy who did Victor's shoes, a real pro. Unfortunately, in addition to beautifully buffed deep mahogany uppers, Victor's guy had polished the leather soles as well. And the soles, about as thick as a blade of grass, were now as slick as well-waxed skis.

They launch their attack from the top of the hill, now walking briskly until they reach an icy patch—then gliding fitfully on their Italian soles and picking up speed as they approach their targets, who never see them coming. Wiseguy One glides smack into Benny, falls and cracks his head on the curb, and Benny is amazed at the amount of blood. The one with the bat winds up for a swing at Carmine, but loses his footing and the bat flies into the air.

Carmine hesitates. He feels a force surge through his body, an almost mystical super power, and he moves mechanically, picking up the bat, raising it into the air, and swinging it at the wiseguy, who slips and slides when he tries to get up. Camine swings the bat, again and again, and the snow is stained with blood and bone. Then he turns to Benny, and raises the bat again.

25

"So now we're dealing with the Russians." Ken Schneider gazed out his office window onto Third Avenue traffic, which was still relatively light at seven a.m. "Geez, these windows are filthy."

He turned to Oberlin and D'Angelo. "What I want to know is, why?"

Oberlin and D'Angelo exchanged a look.

Oberlin said, "Probably the weather."

"What?"

"They can't work."

"Who?"

"The window washers."

"I'm talking about the Russians! How long have they been working with the LCN?"

D'Angelo shrugged. "We haven't been following them."

"Why the hell not?"

"You said the Russians weren't our concern."

Schneider turned to Oberlin. "Did I say that?"

"I don't know, I wasn't there that day."

"Where were you?"

"Listening to Sandra Benigno telling me that Victor's involved with the Russian mafia."

"Ah."

Ken Schneider settled heavily into a chair at the head of the conference table. Oberlin and D'Angelo sat on opposite sides. "Okay," said Ken. "Which one of you wants to start?"

D'Angelo said, "It's your story, Mark."

Oberlin laid out the details as he understood them from his conversations with Benny, Carmine, and especially Sandra B.

"The KGB has been actively surveilling the Odessa Mafia, determined to repatriate every piece of artwork that was smuggled out of Russia since the revolution. Odessa is having trouble monetizing these pieces because they're listed on every stolen art database, and they're very recognizable. Frankly, no one wants this stuff, and if the Russian mob is stuck with it, they need to find a way to get rid of it."

"Obviously."

"Welll here's something that's not so obvious," said Oberlin. "The Russians are scared shitless of the KGB. They're doing this egg deal with the LCN because they feel safer—and also because Dante Forte is an expert on Russian art."

"How did Dante get involved with the Russians? We took down his art franchise years ago."

"But we never got Dante."

"And he's not afraid of fucking with the KGB?" said Schneider

Oberlin shrugged. "Let's just say he'd rather fuck with the FBI and the KGB than with Victor Benigno."

"Where does Benigno come in?" said Schneider.

"Victor provided the down payment for the egg, because Dante doesn't have that kind of cash."

"What kind of cash are we talking about?"

"A hundred grand up front. Another hundred grand on pickup."

Schneider whistled.

"By the time they dismantle a Faberge Egg it could be worth ten times that amount."

"So, the two familes split the take."

"Split?" D'Angelo laughed. "Dante gets some crumbs, if he's lucky. Victor owns him now."

Schneider looked from one to the other. "Benigno took over Forte?"

Nods from Oberlin and D'Angelo.

"This just happened?"

D'Angelo smirked. "Pretty funny, no? We're busy reorganizing our OC squads, while OC is reorganizing itself."

"Shit!" Schneider slammed his hand on the table, then regrouped. "But— this could be a good thing, right? We can put all our resources into one family." He pulled over a flip chart and turned to a clean sheet.

"Ken, we're already doing that. You just merged our two OC squads." When Schneider looked unsure, Oberlin flipped the chart back to the previous page, and Ken studied it with a nod of recognition.

"Okay, we can use this with just a few tweaks—"

D'Angelo moved the marker away from Schneider's reach. "How about we don't get so hung up on charts."

Schneider aimed his pen at a legal pad instead. "We need a case name."

"Maybe...Operation Egg Drop."

Schneider waited a beat. "Right." He marked the file with the case name and set it aside. "What's our time frame here?"

"Friday two p.m."

"Tomorrow!?"

"Tomorrow's Friday..."

"Tomorrow's *a* Friday! You're sure it's not next Friday."

"I'm sure about the date, Ken."

Schneider closed his eyes as if to make it all go away.

"Ken?"

"Okay, right. So what do we need?"

Oberlin cleared the table in front of him and plotted the likely scenario at the car dealership with sticky notes. "This is the showroom," he said, sticking three notes at the far end of the table. "And let's say this is the lot, with twelve legitimate dealer's BMW's, and the three stolen cars parked among them." Oberlin began to peel and press sticky notes onto the table.

"What are you doing?" D'Angelo said.

"These are the cars."

"But they look exactly like the showroom."

"Use your imagination."

"Oh for God's sake." Schneider jumped up from his chair and pulled over the easel. "See? This is why we need charts."

Five minutes later Operation Egg Drop was charted in full. The Dealership was on the corner of a busy intersection, with entrances on both the highway and side street. The FBI surveillance van would park along the side street where the team would have unobstructed views of the showroom and the lot.

Timing was crucial. Dante was not scheduled to make an appearance until after the two other "customers" had already driven off the lot with their new BMW's. If they allowed the car transfer to take place, and tried to prevent the buyers from escaping by placing roadblocks on the residential side streets, they would spook Dante, and lose the real prize—a Faberge egg.

Instead, they'll place an undercover agent in the lot, milling about with the other customers, before the Russian driver unloads his passengers. Until money changes hands with the manager, The Law can't make a move.

"Who is this manager?" said D'Angelo. "Is he a Mob guy?"

"He's an affiliate. He basically rents out parking spaces to the Russians, and he handles the transactions."

"So he's the one to get," said Schneider.

"Yes, and if we get him, we can bring them all down," said D'Angelo. "He provides the requisite number of spaces for the stolen cars, which can vary, day to day."

"And he puts his dealer plates on these cars?"

Oberlin said, "He uses fake plates. And the Russians have already stamped the cars with new VIN's. The buyers—who are paying around a third less than list—drive the cars home, garage them, then take the bill of sale to the DMV with proof of insurance and re-register them in their own names."

"The manager of the dealership is a very important guy. He knows the names of the sellers and the buyers, and which cars are parked in which spaces—"

"And he knows which of the three cars has the egg," said D'Angelo.

"Exactly." Oberlin smiled at Schneider. "It's like three-card monty."

"Never played it," said Schneider quickly.

"There's a lot of moving parts here," said D'Angelo. "And the timing is tricky. We'll need a surveillance van, a backup car and driver, and three more agents, minimum."

Schneider shook his head slowly. "Has it occured to either of you that this—" he made finger quotes—"auto exchange will take place in broad daylight in the middle of a friday afternoon? When there might be innocent members of the Beemer-buying public milling about."

Oberlin and DeAndrea were silent.

"What happens when we corner these guys? How do we protect the public? This could create a shitload of mayhem, all for the sake of a stolen car ring which— like the Forte operations—will just gather itself up, dust itself off and set up operations somewhere else."

Oberlin sat back and drummed his fingers on the table. "You, Ken, would be responsible for taking down an auto theft ring, an art smuggling cartel—and Victor Benigno. This will make your career."

Schneider shook his head. "My career's been made. I'm retiring next year, gentlemen."

"Yeah," said D'Angelo. "So why not go out on a high note?"

"Tom's right," said Oberlin. He gathered his sticky notes from the conference table, balled them up, and tossed them into the waste paper basket, adding, "It's worth a shot."

Schneider looked at Oberlin. "We need informant statements, Mark. I assume we can speak with your TEI's before the egg drops?"

Oberlin shuffled his feet under the table.

"Mark?"

"Yeah, but I need to find them first."

"Find them?" Schneider stared hard at Oberlin. "You mean to say, you've lost Benny Cataldo?"

"Just for the moment. Don't worry, Ken. He'll turn up." But even as Oberlin reassured his SAC, he wasn't sure himself. After all, wasn't Oberlin the one who told Benny he was cutting him loose? That's a scary prospect for an informant, and Oberlin hadn't really meant it, but how could Benny know that.

Rats were people too, after all. Carmine had come to his aid with considerable risk to his own life, and Benny had helped to save Carmine's life, when he could have just stepped back into the shadows. One of them, he wasn't sure which, was indirectly responsible for Hayford Semple's death. But they didn't put the gun in his hand and fire it. Hay was a victim of his own romantic attachment to a doomed mobster. Benny and Carmine were just rats doing their rat jobs and trying to make their way in the world, with their own rat hopes and dreams.

Now, It was time to think like a rat.

Back in his office he called Benny's repair shop and let the phone ring twice—their code for requesting a callback. Oberlin waited the stipulated two minutes, and then dialed Carmine's number at the bakery. The phone was answered on the first ring.

"Look, just leave a number, I gotta call you back. I'm covered in flour here."

Oberlin said, "Lorena?"

"Who the hell else would it be?"

"I was looking for Carmine."

"So was I. Good luck." Then, "Who is this?"

"Mark Oberlin."

"Oh, the FBI agent," she muttered. "He's not here, and I don't think he's coming back. What's another way of saying he's gone into hiding? Riding away on an animal—"

"Er...he's on the lam?"

"Yeah, that's it."

"What makes you think he's hiding, Mrs. Rizzo?"

"He left a note. Last night. Look, I gotta go. My bread is rising and I gotta fill the canolli."

The line went dead. Oberlin replaced the handset and the phone rang immediately. He picked up and said briskly, "Oberlin."

There was the sound of breathing.

"Benny?" he said.

More breathing.

"Carmine?" When there was no response Oberlin barked, "Who the hell is this?"

"B-Billy. Billy Benigno." He sounded breathless. "I need to tell you something."

"Okay, sure. Where are you?"

"At the gas station near my house. I ran up here...need your help."

141

"Okay," said Oberlin. "First, take a breath." He heard a sharp inhale and waited a few seconds before adding, "You can let it out now Billy."

A long swooshing sound. "Okay, thanks," said Billy. "I'm calm now. Listen, I think my mom's in trouble."

"With who? Your father?"

"Not yet, but maybe soon."

"Go on."

"Lisa saw my mom give her keys to a stranger at Bloomingdales."

Oberlin's back stiffened.

"She asked my mom about that, because they were fighting over me, and my mom said the man was a parking attendant and Lisa didn't believe her and..."

"And?"

"And she told her father. She told Dante."

Silence, then Oberlin said, "So...do you think Dante would say something to your father? And he would think—"

"She's having an affair. Yes, that's what he would think." Moments passed. "We have to tell him the truth."

"Which truth?"

"That it was you. She was meeting you at Bloomingdales."

"Hold on, Billy. Hold on." Oberlin gathered his thoughts. "What makes you think it was me?"

A laugh. "I'm a kid, Agent Oberlin. Not an idiot."

"Billy, of course it was me..."

"In a bad disguise..."

Oberlin winced.

"...and now my mother might be in trouble all because I agreed to help *your* informant. And *she* agreed to help *you*!"

"Because she was worried about *you*, Billy. That's how this whole thing started. Look, we're getting down to the wire on this—"

"I know. Tomorrow afternoon at Dan's Driveaway—"

"And you are not, I repeat, *not*, to be anywhere near the place."

"What about my mom?"

"I'll keep her safe. That's a promise."

Silence.

"Billy? Did you hear what I said?"

"Yeah."

"So just stay home tomorrow."

"Do you think anyone could get killed?"

"No. And I'll make sure no one even gets hurt," Oberlin made the promise with no idea how he would keep it.

"There's one other thing you should know, Agent Oberlin."

"Yes?"

"Lisa was adopted. She told me. Dante thinks no one knows, and he wants to keep it that way."

"But Sandra—your mother— doesn't know this, right?"

"She doesn't know anything about the adoption because no one is supposed to know. She told Dante that she's positive he's my father."

"You know, he can get proof that he isn't."

A pause. Then, "Agent Oberlin. If my father finds out they were together when my mom was with my father, he'll kill them both. Whether or not Dante knocked up my mom. I gotta go."

"Stay home tomorrow," said Oberlin into the dead receiver. "I'll take care of your mom."

Daybreak at the Benigno cul de sac.

The snowy landscape revealed nothing of the overnight carnage. The curb at the bottom of the hill, recently covered with blood, had been refreshed with a thin layer of powder. Even the hillside had been wiped clean of fine leather footprints and skidmarks.

So maybe, Carmine thought as he surveyed the site, it had all been a dream.

"Nothing," he whispered.

"Nothing?"

"Yeah, take a look." Carmine passed the binoculars to Benny.

Camouflaged in white painters' coveralls, they had returned to the scene with Benny's binoculars and Carmine's Kodak Instamatic, a gift from his wife. There was nothing to photograph, so Carmine didn't bother removing it from the box where it had lurked, undisturbed, since his birthday five years ago.

"Wh-where are those guys?"

"Victor—"

"Maybe they left—"

"He cleaned it all up." Benny shook Carmine's shoulder. "Victor was here already. He cleaned up the mess."

"B-but, now there's *nothing* to show the Russians," said Carmine bitterly. "What are they gonna do? Just take our word for it that we're changing teams? We're desperate now, Benny. They'll know. They'll smell it before we even walk in the door..."

"Calm down..."

"And all because you were supposed to kill me..."

"I still might..."

"And now...now we've killed two of Victor's men—and we can't even prove it."

"Carmine," said Benny urgently. "Let's get the fuck out of here."

They hiked to Carmine's brother-in-law's car, which was parked about a mile away, in a tidy, unremarkable subdivision.

While they sat there, trying to figure out next steps, the workday was beginning, and homeowners headed for their cars, preparing for the daily commute. One man, his overcoat unbuttoned and a newspaper under his arm, paused outside his car, then walked in their direction.

"Shit," said Benny.

The man rapped lightly on the driver's side window, and Benny lowered it a couple of inches. "All okay in there?"

"Yeah, fine. Just having a little trouble getting it started."

"Ah, okay. I saw the windows fogged up." He turned to go, then added, "Hey, didn't mean to intrude..."

"Oh—ha ha," said Carmine, too brightly. He turned the ignition key, easily starting the car. "Have a great day," he called as he raised the window and pulled away from the curb, trying to avoid the feet of the good samaritan who made no move to get out of the way. "What a stunad," Carmine muttered, gunning the engine for a few yards, then slowing down to a crawl. "So where are we going now?"

"This job happens tomorrow. We gotta find the Russian boss."

"But we don't know where he is. We don't even know *who* he is!"

"Yeah, but I know who does. Make a left at the corner. We're going to Yonkers."

"What's in Yonkers?"

"Dan's DriveAway Dealership."

Carmine turned left at the corner. The good samaritan from the neighborhood jotted down Carmine's brother-in-law's license plate number in his pocket diary, and tucked it back in his pocket.

Benny spotted the small triangle flags lining the L-shaped lot of the car dealer. "That's it. Pull up in front of the showroom," he instructed Carmine.

On the way, they had stopped at a diner for breakfast, since the dealer didn't open until 10 am. Carmine had been grumbling about having to use the bathroom as soon as they resumed their drive to Yonkers, but Benny wouldn't let him make another stop. "They better have a john," said Carmine.

"He's not gonna have a public toilet," said Benny. "Just park in front of the door. You can go to the gas station across the street, and I'll wait here until you get back."

Carmine parked, then bolted from the car and staggered over to the service station like a drunk trying to hold his liquor. It was a few minutes before ten, opening hour, and Benny hunkered down in his seat while he watched the early activity in the showroom. A fashionably dressed young woman was holding out a clipboard for a middle aged man in a well tailored suit. The man looked at it, glanced out at the parking lot—causing Benny to sink even lower in his seat—and then returned his attention to the clipboard.

Carmine took care of business at the Service Station toilet, and stopped to buy cokes for himself and Benny. His spirits lifted with the grey clouds of the preceding days, and as he made his way back to the dealership he considered the events of the night before—the trouble he had avoided and then caused, and the consequences he and Benny might face. The thing that niggled away at him, the intrusive little thought that he had not been able to chase away, was that maybe, just maybe, Benny was not as smart as he claimed to be.

Maybe Benny, who was supposed to save their asses, had no idea what the fuck he was doing. Like now, instead of waiting for Carmine to return, Benny was already in the showroom, in front of some suit's face, trying to get him to stop shaking his head as he indicated Carmine's brother-in-law's car parked just outside the glass doors. Carmine straightened up, took a breath, and joined Benny in the showroom.

"Oh, here he is," said Benny, draping a friendly arm around Carmine's neck. "Meet Mr. Orlov."

Carmine whispered through gritted teeth, "Are we using our real names?"

"This is Stan. Stan Lowsky," said Benny, without breaking his tight smile. After a nudge from Benny, Carmine extended his hand. "Nice to meet you Mr. Orlov."

"Same here," Orlov grunted. "Look, I told your friend…uh, sorry, what was your name?"

"Ben…son. Jim Benson."

"Yeah, as I told Mr. Benson, I'm not taking on any more used cars this month, and especially not a Camaro."

"Okay, fine," said Carmine. "Let's go…"

"Wait, Mr. Orlov," said Benny. "Sometimes we find outselves in a situation where we have cars more up your alley. More up to your standards, like BMW's."

Orlov eyed them both warily. The showroom was starting to get busy, with sales reps arriving, and browsers from the lot coming indoors to ask for demos and details about the cars. "Who recommended me? Where did you get my name?"

"Let's just say we have some friends in Brighton Beach."

At the mention of Brighton Beach Mr. Orlov's face turned pale. "I don't know anyone in Brighton Beach, gentlemen. I'm afraid you're completely off base here. But why not go across the street to the Chevy dealership, see if you'll have more luck there." Then he added, "But wait, let me make a phone call for you, so you don't waste your time. How's that?"

"Much appreciated!" Benny said enthusiastically

"I'll be back in a minute." The manager walked to the back of the showroom and ducked into his office, closing the door. He picked up the phone and punched in a number, then turned his back to the glass wall. "Two men," he said in Russian. He waited, then repeated in a whisper, "KGB?" Then, "I know, I know it's possible. They're not Russian, though…yes I know they hire non-Russian spies." After a moment, "Yes, I understand. We cancel the pickups. Nothing moves in or out of the lot until further notice." He was about to hang up, then repeated, "Yes, of course I'll take down the plate number."

Mr. Orlov planted a fake smile on his face and walked quickly back to the showroom. "I'm sorry, no luck," he said with a shrug. "It was…a longshot, as they say." He summoned his assistant. "Please excuse me, I've got work to do."

The men left the showroom, Benny deflated, and Carmine suddenly anxious about the car. "I gotta get this back to my brother-in-law."

"Now?" says Benny.

"Yeah, before he reports it missing."

"Maybe he already has."

"Nah, my wife wouldn't let him do that."

"What do we do for wheels? Oberlin's got eyes on our own cars by now."

"Yeah, lemme think—I'll give this car back and ask Lorena if I can borrow hers. She knows I'm having a little trouble, gotta keep out of sight."

Benny stared hard at his companion. "Won't the Feds be tracking her car too?"

"Oh, yeah. Wait. Maybe Mo'll lend me his car."

"Mo? Who's Mo?"

"My wife's Aunt's cousin's brother. Cosmo."

Benny processed this. "Your wife has a big family."

"She does."

"And she'd do this for you? Get her aunt's cousin's brother to lend you his car?"

"Sure."

"Wow," said Benny, truly impressed. "You two have the strangest marriage."

"Tell me about it."

Back in Brighton Beach, the Russians in the chop shop have been planning their next move. Around the corner, in a white delivery van that's been parked on the street overnight, two female KGB agents turn off their surveillance equipment. They pull away from the curb and head for Lorena Rizzo's Arthur Avenue bakery.

"Never seen that before." Benny watched in fascination as two women pulled away from the curb in front of the bakery.

"Never seen what?" said Carmine, slipping easily into the vacated space.

"Women driving a van."

"Where have you been, Rip Van Winkle." Carmine turned off the engine and sat back in his seat hard, as if to merge his body with the car's. "Remember, let me do the talking."

"Your wife hates me, Carmine. Why don't I just wait here?"

"Because she'll see you sitting out here and wonder why you won't come in."

"Nah, she'll be happy we're getting along."

Benny scrutized Carmine, like a zoologist discovering a new species. "What are we…in kindergarten?"

"Trust me. She'll be happy I'm not in trouble by myself."

"So, she knows you're in trouble?"

"Yes."

"How much have you told her?"

"Nothing much. Just that I didn't think I would survive past Wednesday night."

"But you didn't tell her why."

Carmine shook his head. "The less she knows, the better."

Benny still couldn't process this level of care and devotion to one's reviled partner. "Okay, I'll come in."

At two p.m. the store was empty. Lorena was tossing malformed bread loaves and day old pastry into a bag for the charity pickup. She glanced up briefly when they came through the door, then resumed her task until the bag was full. "We better talk in the office," she said.

Carmine, and a reluctant Benny, followed Lorena into the small, yeasty smelling office at the back of the bakery. She shut the door and turned to Carmine, ignoring Benny completely. There was fear in her eyes. "They're looking for you."

"Who?" said Carmine.

"Two women with foreign accents, maybe Polish or Russian, I can't tell the difference. They just left, not ten minutes ago."

Benny said, "Did you see what kind of car they were driving?"

"Yeah. A white van."

"We pulled into their space just now," said Carmine.

"Did they see you?"

"I don't think so. What did they want?"

"They said you might be looking for a car service." Lorena put hands on hips defiantly. "What do young foreign women have to do with car services, Carmine?"

"What?"

"You heard me. What services are they really providing?"

Benny put his hand to his mouth to cover a smile.

"And you're in on it too. You were always the bad influence, Benny." She took a step toward him and he took a step back. "You wanted him dead so you could collect life insurance!"

"Yeah, but so did you!" he shouted back.

"That's different. I'm his wife!"

"Okay, okay," said Carmine, ever the peacemaker. "Look, I came to give back your brother's car…"

149

"How nice of you."

"And to see if I can possibly borrow your Aunt's cousin's brother's car."

"Mo's?"

Carmine nodded, and winced, expecting a verbal blow. Instead, Lorena said, "Yeah, he's not using it now anyway. I got another delivery service."

"Thanks, I'll make it up to you Lorena."

"Yeah, sure." She seemed to soften. Benny watched, transfixed by this marital theatre, as she added, "I don't know what trouble you're in, Carmy. But when it's all over, you're welcome to come back to the bakery." She reached into the pocket of her apron and pulled out a business card. "Those women said to give you this."

Camine put the card in his jacket pocket. "I'll tell you all about it as soon as the smoke clears. So, can I have the keys?"

"Oh, yeah." She pulled a set of keys from a hook on the wall near the door. "The van's parked around the corner."

Benny looked from one to the other. "It's a van?"

They nodded.

Benny nodded along with them. "What color? Wait…let me guess."

They nodded encouragingly.

"White?"

"Bingo!" said Lorena.

Benny grumbled and slammed the door of the van as he got out.

"What's your problem?" said Camine. "At least it's wheels."

"It's a van, you moron! A white van!"

"So? Lot's of vans are white."

"So we're a moving target if the Feds mistake our van for the Russian's van."

"First of all, we don't know who those women are."

"They're Russians! Orlov from the dealership probably called them. How else would they have tracked down your brother's sister's aunt's—"

"My brother-in-law's."

"Jeez—the car!"

"And second of all," Carmine continued, "The feds don't make those kinds of mistakes."

Benny jammed his hand into Carmine's jacket pocket and pulled out the business card.

"Hey! What the f—"

"They're contacts, Carmine. It's what we've been looking for. Russian contacts." He peered at the card. Nothing was printed on it except a phone number, in a very small font, in the lower right corner. "Let's find a place to stay tonight. I'll give these gals a call, and we'll be in bed with them by tomorrow morning." When Carmine looked horrified he added, "Just a figure of speech, Carmy. Believe me."

26

Friday morning at the Benigno house was barely-contained chaos.

Victor had spent much of the pre-dawn hours outside, supervising the cleanup of his two dead soldiers. This turn of events was disappointing and inconvenient, but Victor consoled himself with the fact that even though his soldiers were not the intended victims, the resulting body count was the same. Instead of burying Benny Bianco and Carmine Rizzo, two top rats who were obviously not as stupid as they looked, his loyal men were burying two of their own.

He sighed. He felt something shift in his gut when he thought about Sal and Vinny. They had been proud that he, *the Boss*, had let them use his shoe shine guy. He thought maybe he should have asked his men to remove their shoes, but nah. What would he, Victor, do with them? Hang them from his rear view mirror? Have them bronzed, like they did with Billy and Clara's baby shoes?

"Whaddaya gonna do," he said softly. "Business is business."

After a hot shower, he turned off the tap and stayed inside the stall to preserve as much warmth as possible. He towel dried quickly in the remaining heat of the bathroom, and walked naked to his wardrobe, where he examined himself in the mirrored armoire. He sucked in his gut, flexed his still-articulated sixty-five year old biceps and triceps, and wondered what the future would bring.

This being Victor Benigno, the future consisted of next minutes and next moves, rather than any deep dive into the meaning of life. He was a practical man, with practical needs, some of them pressing. Like now, for instance, his only thought was pressing his body, and his manhood, into the obliging crevices of Vera K. He smiled when he thought of how Sandra referred to his mistress as Miss Poland, had no idea where that had come from, since Vera had never been a beauty contestant—wasn't even beautiful, not like Sandra.

He finished dressing, dark wool trousers, and a light gray half-zip sweater, not cashmere, but a heavy merino wool. *Leaves fewer stray fibers, less evidence of womanizing for Sandra to find.*

"Dad! Phone!" Clara's voice broke the spell. "It's Mr. Forte."

Victor looked at his watch, mumbled "shit," then called down from the top of the stairs, "Tell him I'll be there in ten minutes. Running a little late." He grabbed his wallet from the dresser and went down, taking each step with a plodding determination, and hesitating in the stairwell. "What happened to the Bay of Naples?" he said to no one in particular. Then he shrugged, grabbed his car keys from an ornate Venetian side table, and left the house.

Billy and his mother paused their arguing at the sound of the door slamming shut, then resumed.

"I want you home after school. You are to come directly home."

"I can be here by four…"

"You get out at 2:30. I want you home at 3."

"Why?"

"Because!" Sandra paused, figured this would not be enough, and added, "I'm going out, and Clara will be here by herself."

"I'm fine by myself!" Clara's voice pierced through the closed door of her bedroom. "I'm not a baby!"

"Why can't you do this for me, just this once," she complained to her son. "What are you doing that's so important you can't be here for your sister?"

"I don't need anyone here for me!" called Clara.

Sandra and Billy looked at each other, then shouted toward the stairs, "Shut up, Clara!"

"I could ask you the same question, mom," said Billy.

"What question?"

"What's so important that you have to go out this afternoon, on a

Friday when you usually stay home and make us fish sticks and pizza. Your canasta game is Tuesdays."

Sandra's mouth dropped. She wasn't expecting to need an alibi for her son. "Don't compare us, William! I can come and go as I please! And If I please to play cards this afternoon—"

"If it pleases you—"

"Yeah, thanks, wise-guy with the grammar lessons. I can play cards any day I want. And I can still be home in time to make fish sticks and pizza."

Billy's brain seemed to be battling two conflicting thoughts. Finally, with a slight smile, he said, "You're right, mom. I can be home right after school for Clara."

"Oh, Billy, thank you. You have no idea what this means to me."

She leaned over to give him a peck on the cheek, and Billy said, "So you're going to a card game, right?"

"Yes, of course."

"Where?"

"Aunt Rose." This was Sandra's sister, one town away.

"What time do you expect to be home—just so I can leave the house neat for you. You know what a slob Clara can be—"

Clara appeared at the top of the stairs. "I heard that Billy! I hate you!"

"She doesn't really hate you," whispered Sandra. "She loves her brother."

Billy and Clara got dressed, ate some pop tarts, and waited by the front door for the school bus. Sandra said, "I'm going food shopping. I'll see you after school."

"After your card game."

"Yeah, when cards are over, about four, maybe five, depending on traffic."

"Aunt Rose is ten minutes away. What kind of traffic are you expecting?"

"Oh, leave me alone!" blurted Sandra.

She clicked across the slate walkway on her three-inch slingback pumps, opened the garage door with the remote, and settled into the Caddy. After adjusting the mirror, to examine her face, she put the car in reverse and backed out, side-swiping the mirror and cursing all the way to the street.

She put the car in drive and waited, gathering her thoughts, trying to put seeming contradictions to rest. She was going shopping. This much was true. As for the card game, Billy was right. There had been a moment during their heated discussion when she thought maybe he would come home from school instead of heading for the car dealership this afternoon. But the little smile on Billy's face, a signal that he was getting away with something, changed her mind.

She didn't want to go to this criminal meet and greet at Dan's Driveaway. She didn't want to throw herself in front of her son to protect him from Dante—or from Victor. But because of that smile, she knew that this was where he would be when the action began. She stopped at the service station in the supermaket strip mall, and said to the attendant, "Filler up."

She paid the attendant and waited at the pump until he walked away. Then, ignoring the honk from the car behind her, she checked out her makeup in the rearview mirror. "Okay, okay!" She muttered. Then, as an afterthought, she pulled open the glove compartment and felt around for her pistol. Check. She pulled away from the pump and flipped a finger at the car behind her.

Billy and Clara took the same bus to different schools. She sat behind him and got out first, ramming a knuckle into his head before racing down the aisle for the door. He ignored her and fixed his hair, plotting his next moves.

The most important development of this day, to Billy's teenage mind and groin, was that both of his parents would be out of the house for the whole afternoon, his father on an auto theft job, and his mother sneaking around the Dealership to make sure he, Billy, would be okay. Billy had promised Oberlin he would stay away from the place, and Oberlin had assured him that he would protect his mother, in fact, make sure that no one was killed or hurt.

Billy was worried about his mother, but not as much as before his talk with Oberlin. Simply put, he was respecting the wishes of them both. Victor would take care of business, enlist a couple of men— maybe his favorites, Sal and Vinny. Of course, Dante Forte would attend.

That meant Lisa would be free to hang out at Billy's soon-to-be empty house. He'd get her to skip afternoon classes, and either lock Clara out of the house, or bribe her with a box of mallomars when she got home.

Dante Forte sat at a round table in the darkened interior of Sorrento Di Sera, a stucco-clad rectangle of a restaurant at the end of a strip mall.

He looked at his watch while the waiter poured out two glasses of water. Regular hours started at 6 pm, but the owner opened at all hours for Family guys, on very little notice. "Would you like to hear the specials, while you wait?" said the owner/waiter.

"You can skip the antipasti. Too early."

"Okay, then for pasta, we have—"

"It's nine a.m., George. Who eats pasta at nine a.m.?"

"Mr. Benigno."

"Really? What does he usually order?"

"Spinach gnocchi. With a fried egg on top."

"Ah."

"Makes it more breakfasty."

"Okay. We'll both have that." George retreated backwards, and Dante added, "And don't wait to put the order in."

"Into where? It's just me!" George said with a laugh, and thinking: *You got me here at all hours, trying to accommodate you sleazebags. I got a family and a life too.* Still, it was too late to change the relationship, and hard not to love the extra bucks they floated his way.

"Okay, George. So *you* can go boil the gnocchi and fry the eggs," replied Dante, and he flicked a couple of bills across the table. Everyone had a hand out these days. George's restaurant depended on patrons like Victor, himself and the boys, especially since they had managed to scare away any normal, non-mob customers.

"Thank you, Mr. Forte." George gathered up the cash and set off for the kitchen.

Dante looked up with a start, to find Victor looming over him, suddenly, as if he had descended from the ceiling. "Victor, so good to see you," he said, thinking *sonofabitch for making me wait so long.*

"So I'm a little late," Victor replied tightly, reading Dante's thoughts. He looked around the small, empty dining room.

"We're alone, Vic," said Dante reassuringly.

"Yeah." But Victor seemed nervous, off his game this morning. "You know, I had to do some early morning landscaping," he said, nodding, Dante nodding along with him. "When it rains, it pours."

Dante could not make the connection between the landscaping activities, i.e. getting rid of bodies, and this aphorism. This was frequently the case when Victor tried to be cryptic. "Things happen. What can you do?" He offered.

"I'm not blaming myself," replied Victor, sharply.

"No, of course not."

"It's this deal, my friend. I think it's cursed. And I blame that little rat Benny for the whole thing."

"Rats are rats. It's what we have to deal with." *You tried to fuck him, and he returned the favor.*

Victor looked at Dante for a moment. "Tell me, truthfully. Did he ever try to screw you over when he was working for you?"

Dante narrowed his eyes, uncomprehending. He was thinking, *you dumbass,* but deferring to mob protocol he replied, "Well, he did jump ship and go to my only competitor...if that qualifies."

"Yeah? Where'd he go?"

"Er...to your organization."

Victor nodded, "Right, right." Then, "The pickup this afternoon. How can we be sure Bianco and his piece of shit sidekick Rizzo haven't queered this deal?"

Victor looked toward the kitchen, and Dante made room on the table for the breakfast platters headed their way. George quickly set them down and scurried away without a word. "My favorite. Very thoughtful of you, Dante."

"Of course. But back to our boys. They murdered two of your best last night. They're long gone by now. And you can forget about them going to the feds."

"Yeah, that's right," said Victor, a piece of spinach hanging from his lip. "Even if Rizzo says they killed two guys in self defense...there's no bodies!" He let out a laugh. He chewed on another piece of gnocchi and turned serious. "I liked those two guys."

"Yes, quality people. Sal and..."

"Vinny. Salvatore and Vincenzo. I made peace with their loved ones, very expensive."

"Young guys, huh. With wives, and kids?"

"No. Still living at home."

"Ah. And their parents—"

"I told you, I expressed my sympathies in a very meaningful and expensive way."

"So very good of you, Victor." *For sending their sons on a suicide mission.*

"Okay, enough with the schmaltz. Business is business. Tell me again about this precious art I'm buying."

"It's a Faberge Egg, Victor."

"I'm buying an egg? Are you nuts? Did we actually discuss this when I laid out a hundred grand?"

Dante dabbed his mouth genteely with his cloth napkin. "I told you it was a piece of artwork, Victor."

"Here I am thinking I'm buying a masterpiece, like my Bay of Naples."

Dante's eyes widened. "Bay of Naples? Not Renoir..."

"What? No—

"Is it a print? Lithograph? Numbered series?"

"I'm pretty sure it's original." Victor's voice was tentative.

"Bruegel the Elder?"

"Who the fuck is that?"

"Then which artist, Victor?"

"Antonia. Antonia LaRosa."

Dante sat back in his chair. "I'm not familiar with her work."

"Why would you be? She's my wife's sister's husband's cousin." Victor watched Dante deflate. He never understood these artsy people. He understood that people might pay a high price for original art from dead people, but he didn't see the appeal of the art itself. "Let's get back to the egg." Victor looked at him steely-eyed. "You said you had a reliable fence."

Dante hesitated. "Actually, I said I had a way to monetize it."

"So what's the plan? You have a buyer already?"

"Not exactly. Not in the egg's present form."

Victor pushed his plate away and leaned in hard, his chest resting on his forearms. "What the fuck is that supposed to mean? Not in its present form...we wait until it hatches?"

Dante, thinking *what a moron,* said, "The egg, as such, is too recognizable to be fenced. These eggs are rare artifacts in the world of art. In fact, there's a database of stolen and missing eggs, on which this appears."

"Speak English. How do I make money on it?"

"I have a jeweler friend," said Dante, glancing toward the door as if expecting him to appear. "He can dismantle the egg, take it apart, gem by gem, and sell the parts for us easily through his contacts." When Victor still looked bored, Dante added, "The artisans used only flawless stones, Victor. Would you like to hear a bit of Faberge history?"

Victor growled, "No," then added after a moment of reflection, "So this friend of yours...he runs a chop shop for jewelry."

"Instead of cars. Yes, exactly."

Dante shifted in his chair and stole a glance at his Rolex. It was exhausting, as well as pointless, to discuss art with this *cretin.* He hoped the egg would somehow escape Victor's ignorant clutches and survive this criminal adventure intact. But Dante *himself* was hoping to survive this criminal adventure intact. He added with fake enthusiasm, "So this would be quite a haul for you, Victor."

"For us, Dante," Victor replied, with a serpentine smile. "We got a partnership, remember. We're joined at the hip."

Dante remembered. Of course he did. He remembered the meeting where this was announced, and when Victor's goon pulled out a gun and pumped a couple of bullets into one of Dante's best soldiers. To prove he was top dog, to hammer home the point that Dante would be working for *him,* Victor ordered Dante to clean up the scene, body and all. He shuddered. Crossing Victor was out of the question, and the thought of it kept him up at night, especially since the school parking lot run-in with his crazy wife Sandra.

About two miles away from Sorrento Di Sera, Benny and Carmine are cruising slowly through the outskirts of town, looking for a suitable phone booth for calling the Russian mobsterettes.

Benny is now driving, and Carmine, feeling safe and sound with Benny at the helm of this Russian auto scam, fidgets with the radio, tuning from static to news and back to static, until the AM dial finds a very narrow band of music.

"Here we go," says Benny, pulling into a service station. "Do you see a phone booth?"

Carmine shrugs. "Maybe it's inside."

"Ok, wait here."

"Hold on," says Carmine, turning off the radio. "What are you gonna say to them? We can't tell them too much, you know, I mean, about the past couple of days."

Benny faces him, with an eyeroll and a sigh. "Do you think I'm stupid, Carmine?"

"I just—"

"No. Do you think I haven't thought this thing out?"

Carmine shrugs and sits back in his seat, defeated. "Never mind. Of course I don't think you're stupid."

"That's right, Carmine. I'm not stupid. And that's why I'm a survivor. Get it, Carmine? I'm a survivor, so just stick with me."

"Yeah, great. Just go make the call."

Benny uses his last coins on the phone call. When a woman's voice answers, he talks fast. He says he knows about the stolen auto exchange at Dan's Driveaway Dealership, and about the car with the hidden faberge egg. He wants their people to know that the FBI is also aware, so they should be careful.

When there is silence on the other end, Benny thinks he has impressed them, and they are assessing the situation.

"I just gave you a freebie," he says into the phone. "What I, and my partner Carmine want to do, is come to some sort of working arrangement—where we can be your eyes and ears, maybe insulate you from the Feds, and the Benigno family."

He waits. The heavily accented voice says, "Top level of the parking garage at 13-5 River Street. Four o'clock. Don't be late. Come alone."

"With my partner."

"Yes, bring him too. I think we can come to a suitable arrangement."

Benny is pumped. This could turn into a lucrative association going forward, as soon as he's had a chance to study the activities of the Odessa gang, how he can be most helpful, and what he should request in terms of compensation. As for mob retribution, Benny is sure the Russians will be able to "disappear" him and Carmine, since Victor's got eyes and ears everywhere.

"Repeat that address back to me," says the woman.

At that moment the operator asks for more coins, and Benny fumbles in his pocket with one hand, while trying to signal Carmine with the other. But Carmine is preoccupied with the radio and doesn't see him.

The line goes dead. Benny hangs up, checks the change well, and goes back to the car, mumbling "13-5 River Street."

Back in the Bronx, in the bakery on Arthur Avenue, Lorena Rizzo picks up the phone. "Yeah? What can I do for you?"

"Listen to me," comes a heavily accented voice. "We saw you yesterday. We are associates of your husband. Do you remember?"

"Of course I remember," said Lorena. "I gave him your card. Did he contact you? And do you mind telling me what this is about? You know, he's not as active as he once was—if you know what I mean."

"What?"

"Look, we have an open marriage, and I'm pretty liberal when it comes to recreational sex—"

"What?"

Lorena hears muffled whispering on the other end of the line.

"Listen!" The voice is hard and mean. "Find your husband and make sure he knows the address is 13-5 River Street. Four o'clock sharp. And we only want the two of them. No one else must come."

"Yeah, fine." Lorena slams down the phone. The rudeness of these Eastern European sex workers was astounding. What did she think Lorena would do? Pimp out their fuck session to the whole neighborhood?

Lorena busies herself with bakery business, but she can't get that phone call out of her mind. The woman sounded harsh, cruel. And why would they meet in a parking garage instead of a cheap motel with hourly rates.

She grabs a sheet pan lined with cannoli, and slips it into the oven.

27

Peter Orlov checked the locks on the three BMW's that were waiting for pickup in the corner of his lot. He had no idea how long the delay would last, but he had to be ready to get the call from his Russian boss telling him that the coast was clear, after they checked out the two bozos who came to him with a car to fence. It had happened before. Word gets around. And those sellers with their hot car trying to make an easy score were sometimes interviewed by his Russian boss and taken care of in some fashion. All Orlov knew was that he never heard from or saw any of them again. That's the way it would be with these two bozos, who couldn't even get their own fake names straight.

The car doors were all locked, and Orlov was about to return to the showroom when he had second thoughts about the dealer plates. Remove them, or leave them, in the event of a quick return to the status quo. He had customers, now, and foot traffic in the lot was building. The sun was out strong after a couple of snowy January days, and he noted with satisfaction that his workers had done a good job with the snow blowers. Don't leave any melted snow that can refreeze, he had told them. He didn't need customers slipping and suing his boss, the owner of the place, who was spending the winter in Palm Springs. Attracting his bosses' attention to the daily activities of the dealership was the last thing Peter Orlov intended to do. He went back to the showroom and put the three sets of keys in a wooden tray on the corner of his desk.

On a leafy sidestreet near the intersection, a dark grey surveillance van pulls up to the curb, engine idling as if undecided whether to stay, then finally quiet. The view is optimal, for the cameras, with one trained on both entrances to the lot, the main one from the highway, and the smaller, one-lane in each direction, directly across from them on the street. There is an unobstructed view of the main lot, as well as the glass enclosed showroom.

Oberlin is at the wheel, D'Angelo is riding shotgun, and two agents from the newly formed Tech squad are in the back of the van, setting up the cameras, monitors, and recorders. "All that glass. They made it easy for us," muttered one of the techs.

"Maybe they've got nothing to hide," said Oberlin.

"Or," said D'Angelo with a laugh, "maybe they want us to *think* they have nothing to hide."

"You know," said Oberlin. "You don't necessarily have to be a cold-blooded cynic to work in this field."

"Yeah, you do. Especially if you want to outsmart the bad guys." D'Angelo made a show of repositioning his shoulder holster. "It's a crazy world, my friend. You're still young, but you'll find out soon enough."

Oberlin was about to reply when a Cadillac with Dante Forte in the passenger seat, and an unknown adult male at the wheel, pulled up in front of the dealership. Dante got out, and the driver exited the lot on the highway side. "Keep your eyes on him," Oberlin told the crew, as Dante pulled open the glass doors and went into the showroom.

"We've got a good view of him," said one of the tech agents.

"Who wouldn't," said D'Angelo. "The place is like a fucking aquarium." He pulled out his binoculars. "And the guy he's talking to is probably the manager, right?"

Peter Orlov shook his head sympathetically as Dante Forte explained his need to drive away with the partially paid-for stolen car. "I'm sorry, I wish I could help you, but like I said, Mr. Forte. There has been a, what you might call, a fuck-up, involving that particular automobile, and its contents. I cannot release it to you until I get the okay from my superiors."

"Look, Orlov, we've all got…" Dante clearly had a hard time saying *superior* when he referred to the new capo…"people we report to. We are already into this deal for quite a tidy sum, and if the car is on the lot, I must insist that you let me take ownership." He pulled an envelope from his messenger bag. "I've got the rest of the payment right here—plus a small bonus for any inconvenience it might cause back at your headquarters."

Orlov looked from Dante to the envelope and back to Dante. He shrugged. "The best I can do is let you know as soon as I get clearance. There's a decent diner across the road from the lot. You can see it from here," he said pointing to a small, vintage 1950's diner at the corner of the other side street opposite Oberlin's surveillance vehicle. "Go there, have some lunch—"

"I had lunch."

"Okay, so have a snack—look, I don't give a rat's ass whether you go to the diner or not. I'm just trying to help you out. I'd rather not have you hanging around the showroom under the circumstances, if you get my drift."

"Yeah. I get your drift." Dante turned to go, then picked up a copy of Architectural Digest from the coffee table in the middle of the showroom. "How will I know when it's clear?"

"There's a phone on the wall in the entrance to the diner. I have the number. I'll call you there."

D'Angelo's binoculars are trained on Dante Forte as the mobster exits the showroom. "Where's he going?"

"To that diner across the street, looks like," says one of the techs.

Oberlin says, "Do we need to reposition?"

"No, I've got him on the monitor," says the other tech.

D'Angelo turns to Oberlin. "You're sure the pick-ups are in the Dealership lot?"

"Based on original intel, yes."

"But things can change, right?"

"Yes, but—"

"This whole thing's going to hell," said D'Angelo. "We need Bianco and Rizzo. Where are they?"

"Hold on." Oberlin's attention was now fixed on a red Cadillac El Dorado that entered the lot from the highway intersection. It moved towards the showroom at full speed, coming to a stop within inches of the plate glass facade.

Sandra.

Oberlin watched as she threw open the car door, jumped out, then turned and picked something up from the console. She headed straight to the wirey, balding middle-aged man who was talking to a female assistant in the middle of the floor. She faced him, then followed him to a glass enclosed office. There was a clear view of Sandra from the surveillance van, but Orlov was blocked by a decorative pillar. Sandra reached into her handbag. Oberlin held his breath...then released it, when she pulled out a manilla envelope.

"I haven't seen your husband," said Orlov, glancing at the photo of a smiling Victor Benigno. "Look, lady. He may have told you he was coming here, but look around. He wasn't here before you got here, and he isn't here now."

"You're lying. You're covering up for him."

"Covering—lady, I don't even know who he is!"

"He's Victor Benigno. Does that ring a bell?"

"Benigno...is he related to the gang boss?"

"He IS the gang boss, Mr. Orlov!" She held another photo in front of his face. "And this young man? You gonna tell me he isn't here either?"

Orlov looked at her, stupified. "Look, if they're interested in buying a car, I'll be here all day. Maybe they decided to come later."

In fact, Victor Benigno had no intentions of spending Friday afternoon chasing down a stolen car with a pricey egg inside. He left that to Dante, the art expert. Nope. Victor had the house to himself, since according to Sandra, she was going to be playing cards all afternoon.

"C'mon. Wear the crown," he cooed into Miss Poland's neck, as they lay in post-coital bliss with Victor trying to coax himself back into performance mode.

"Oh stop it, Victor. I'm not really a Polish beauty queen."

Nor was Miss Poland particularly Polish. She was a Russian emigree with a thick Russian accent, but most people in Victor's milieu could not tell the difference. Her years' long relationship with Victor was not without some pleasure, but mostly she was doing it for the money, for any LCN intelligence she could sell to the Odessa family. "Weren't you supposed to be somewhere today on an important assignment, with very great potential?" She asked him, twirling a lock of his chest hair.

"Oof, now you sound like my wife," he said, unwinding from her embrace. "That's a real joy killer."

"Victor…" She touched his arm and he pulled it away. "Aw, c'mon…"

"I don't feel like it anymore."

"Victor!"

They lay next to each other in silence for a moment. Then she sat up. "Okay. I'll get the crown."

Billy Benigno and Lisa Forte were in the downstairs maid's room when they heard the upstairs floorboards creak.

"I thought you said we had the house to ourselves," said Lisa, wide-eyed.

"Yeah, we are. I promise. That was just Clara…"

"Clara's here!?"

"Don't worry. I bribed her with a box of mallomars."

"And if the little piggy ate them all…what then?"

Billy jumped up from the bed. "I'll get her a bag of chips."

"Maybe some soda. She must be pretty thirsty."

But Clara did not receive any additional snack bribes, because as soon as Billy saw Lisa's bare leg poking out from the sheets, he was on her and they were at it again.

"I suppose you haven't seen this man either?" Relentless, Sandra held up a photo of Dante Forte.

"Hm, I saw a man who resembles him," ventured Orlov.

Sandra looked at the photo again. "Okay, so if you added about twenty years to him, would that make a difference?" While waiting for his response, she reached into her bag and pulled out the pistol.

Orlov's eyes widened. He nodded vigorously. "He was here. I have an appointment with him, but we got held up."

"Where is he now?"

"Follow me?" said Orlov tentatively, eyes on the pistol.

167

Sandra tucked the gun back into her bag and followed Orlov to the entrance.

"See that corner diner across the street?" He said, pointing. "I sent him there to wait."

"Wait for what?"

Orlov shook his head. "If Mr. Forte wants to share his business with you, that's up to him."

"I have a gun." Sandra patted her purse. "I think that's up to me."

Orlov looked around the showroom for a solution to his predicament. A few customers were eyeing the newest BMS's, one man stroking the flank of a convertible like a lover. His three salesmen were engaged with customers, leading them from the showroom to the lot where more models were available for test driving. Dan's Driveaway had a reputation for being very liberal with test drives. As long as the cars had dealer plates, he trusted his customers to return them within a reasonable time frame. No one ever crossed the line into grand theft auto, particularly since dealer plates were so easy to track down. Except, of course, for the outgoing cars from his Odessa clients. Those plates were fake — and Orlov had a limitless supply to tack onto the "transitional cars," as he called them.

When Orlov turned his attention back to Sandra, she was heading for the door.

Oberlin and the crew in the surveillance van watched her push open the showroom door and walk purposefully in the direction of the diner. Fortunately, her towering platform heels slowed her down, and Oberlin, jumping out of the van, was able to overtake her on foot. "Sandra, please come with me," Oberlin said, putting himself in front of her and trying to appear more bulky.

"Oh, so here you are at last. What's going on with you people? I thought there was supposed to be a police sting going on here. Why did I even waste my breath telling you about this?"

"Please come with me."

"I gotta find Billy. I don't know where he is. I don't know where Victor is. But I do know where Dante is, and I'm going to have a private word with him."

While Mark Oberlin was trying to coax Sandra off the Dealership premises and into the surveillance van, where he might be able to calm her down, the crew inside the van were taking bets on whether he would succeed.

"Nah, he's too green. He doesn't have the right touch with women," said D'Angelo.

"I'm betting he does it," said one of the tech agents. "It's the innocent looks that get them all the time."

"Not in my experience," mumbled D'Angelo.

The crew in the surveillance van was busy focussing on Oberlin and Sandra B., who had moved through the rows of parked cars and were now standing near the sidewalk. Because of this they did not notice the white van that passed several feet to their left and entered the parking lot. It pulled to the back of the showroom, idled for a moment, then went still. With remarkable choreography, two women in non-descript street clothes emerged at the same time and walked, shoulder to shoulder, up a short ramp on the side of the building and into a steel utility door.

Orlov was on the phone in his office when the women walked in and closed the door behind. "Please, hang up, Mr. Orlov."

Orlov was startled. "Hold on," he said into the phone."

"Hang up now, Mr. Orlov."

The voice, deep but feminine, with a thick Russian accent, belonged to the younger of the two women, who were dressed alike in heavy gabardine trench coats and thick, rubber soled boots. He placed the phone back on the receiver without taking his eyes off them. "What do you want?"

The older woman, with graying hair and a severe expression, like someone who has worked too hard all her life with nothing to show for it, put her finger to her lips before her companion could speak again. "We have come for the egg, Mr. Orlov."

Orlov was relieved, at first. "Oh, so they sent you to take it back while this little problem is resolved?" They looked at him stone faced. "Is that how you know about the egg?" Now he was starting to feel pinpricks of sweat trickle down his back. "Who...who sent you here?"

"We will tell you everything," said the older woman. "But first, can I see the bathroom?"

"See it? Of course, it's in the hallway, first door to your right."

The older woman left, then returned a moment later and whispered something to her companion. She then turned to Orlov. "We must have the egg, Orlov."

"Look, let me talk to the boss—"

"What boss? We don't work for your boss, you fool. We work for the Motherland. We are the KGB. We are charged with repatriating all treasures stolen from the Soviet Union. We know you have a Faberge Egg. In fact we know exactly which egg it is."

Even Orlov didn't know that. He backed slowly toward the door, rapidly assessing his options. If he gave them the egg, the Brighton Beach gang would get him. Who was the greater threat? These were women, one at least in her sixties, and the other somewhat more petite. He could take them, and he had a pistol in his desk drawer. He wouldn't fire it, of course, but it might be enough to scare them away. "The egg is in a safe, and the key to the safe is in my drawer."

"Which drawer?"

He reached across to his top left hand drawer before they could stop him and pulled out the pistol. He pointed it in their general direction. "Look, I'm not giving you the egg. It's been bought and paid for. I suggest you leave quickly and quietly." He added, "And you can tell *your* boss that things just didn't go the way you planned."

"He will not be happy to hear that, I'm afraid," said the younger woman, moving slowly to his right side, while he trained the gun on the older woman.

"Don't move!" But before he had time to reposition himself, she had slipped behind him like a passing cloud. He felt the sharp stab at the base of his neck and his free hand swatted feebly at the air before his knees buckled, and he went down. "Let's move him. Now!"

The two women left the building through the utility door. Once outside they feigned conversation with each other as they walked, unhurried, to their car. No one noticed them, especially not the agents in the surveillance van, who were training all their resources on the door to the diner. Because when Dante emerged and walked back to the dealership, that would be their signal that the exchange was about to take place.

Oberlin had spent the past fifteen minutes trying to reassure Sandra that neither Billy nor Victor had shown up on their surveillance screens—and that the likelihood of the FBI missing any suspicious activity was very low.

The van was getting stuffy, and Sandra's Eau de Givenchy wasn't helping matters. "Can we open a window?" said a Tech agent.

"No, just turn on ther air," said Oberlin.

"The air?" D'Angelo and the tech agents laughed. "There's no *air*, my friend. This is the FBI in the year 1980. We're still using walkie talkies—"

"Ha! At least we've moved up from tin cans and string!" One Techie laughed loudly at his own joke. The other shook his head, and the van became quiet. Until Sandra spoke.

"So, this is all we got for the grand theft auto slash art smuggling deal? Just this one measly surveillance van. And exactly—" she counted out, "one, two, three, four FBI agents?"

A call came over the radio. Lorena Rizzo, patched in from HQ.

"Where's Mark?" Her voice was shaky.

"Right here."

"Listen, you need to go ask that manager where Carmine and his idiot friend went after they left the dealership..."

D'Angelo snapped, "We're following protocol here, Mrs. Rizzo—"

"Yeah, while you're following protocol someone's been following my husband. Mark. Mark? Are you there?"

"I'm here."

"Listen. I got a call from these two bimbos who told me to tell Carmine to meet them at the big parking garage on Water Street—"

"Why'd they call you?"

"Because the phone—never mind why! It doesn't matter! They're supposed to meet at 4:00."

"Okay, we'll send someone."

"Right away!"

Oberlin hung up the handset. "I think it's time for a chat with Mr. Peter Orlov."

"You're gonna blow our cover," said D'Angelo. "Let's wait until he makes a move."

But Peter Orlov would be making no more moves, at least not on his own. His lifeless body was draped unceremoniously across the toilet in the men's room outside his office, his foot positioned as a doorstop if anyone tried to enter.

"Oh, sorry," said Roger Pine, encountering such resistance as he looked for his boss. Roger was twenty-one and new at the car sales game. His father knew the owner of Dan's Driveaway. In fact, they were both wintering in Palm Springs at the moment, and Roger was excited to be close to a sale, giving his dad bragging rights and making Dan happy that he had hired his friend's kid.

"Mr. Orlov?" Roger had looked in his office before trying the men's room. Now he went back to the office and searched Orlov's desktop for car keys. He pulled a set from the wooden tray, checked the label, then scooped up all three sets and slipped them into his navy blazer pocket.

When he returned to the lot, the young nice-looking couple was hovering over the green BMW, just where he had left them.

"So, can we try it out?" said the young man.

"Why not?" In his excitement, Roger struggled with the sets of keys, until he finally found the one that fit. "Bingo!"

"Oh great," said the young man, opening the passenger door for his companion, then pushing past Roger to get into the driver's seat. "I've driven this model before, so I don't need any instructions."

"Yeah, well," said Roger, whose doubts were rising in proportion to his client's exhuberance. "So, just don't, you know, keep it out too long."

"We won't," said the young man, adjusting the mirrors and not bothering to ask what "too long" might look like.

"There's a full tank of gas," Roger called out, as the bits of remaining asphalt ice spun up into his face. Just as he reached the showroom, Oberlin and D'Angelo raced ahead of him to the door.

They left the body in the bathroom exactly as they had found it. They radioed for ambulence and backup, identified themselves to the half-dozen staff and customers now in the showroom, including Roger Pine, and ordered them to stay put.

"Why?" someone called out.

"Because," said someone standing nearby, "They found the manager dead, in the bathroom."

An elderly gent, who browsed this showroom every Friday afternoon because he had nothing else to do, added his two cents. "People die in bathrooms all the time. How do you know there's been a crime?"

But instead of its intended effect, to rally the crowd to demand immediate release, his remark elicited side glances and low murmurs.

"What?" he demanded.

"We saw you," said a young woman, "Standing by the bathroom, trying to get in."

"So?"

"And then, we *didn't* see you, which means you went inside."

"Or, maybe I changed my mind," said the gent, amused.

"We'll be taking statements from everyone," said Oberlin. "People who used the bathroom, or saw who went into the bathroom and came out again..."

"I saw a woman in a trench coat and army boots," said Roger Pine. "She came out of Mr. Orlov's office and went to the bathroom — but she didn't go in, she just looked inside."

"Where did she go then?"

Roger Pine shrugged. "No idea. I had customers, and I came back to the office to get keys for a test drive."

Sirens were suddenly sounding from all directions. The local police arrived on scene, then the State troopers, followed by FBI and unmarked official vehicles. There was an ambulence, a medical examiner and people in white coats awaiting further instructions.

"Hope it wasn't just a heart attack," murmured a customer. "Hate to see such a waste of taxpayers' money."

The medical examiner confirmed a puncture wound to Mr. Orlov's neck, and time of death. While the newly arrived FBI agents took statements from the staff and clients, the local police assisted the troopers in creating a crime scene barrier around the entire perimeter of Dan's Driveaway Dealership.

Oberlin and D'Angelo raced back to the surveillance van, pulled away from the curb—narrowly missing a cyclist, who gave them the finger—and headed for the tall parking garage on Water Street. "I'll take your statement back at the office," said Oberlin, glancing at Sandra.

""What?"

"That's right, Sandra. You were in there with Orlov, and maybe the last one to see him alive."

"You gotta be kidding! Mark, that's a joke, right?"

"I never joke, Sandra." Too late, Oberlin realized he'd just quoted Ken Schneider.

"Yeah. Too bad. That's probably why you're still single."

The scene at Dan's now drew bystanders and rubberneckers. There were sirens, lights, police at the local, state and federal levels, and street closures with tie-ups and diversions. Even the rotors of a helicopter could be heard off in the distance.

Yes, this wintry Friday afternoon spectacle was truly something to behold—except if you happened to be sitting alongside Dante Forte at the diner across the street. Dante was facing away from the highway, and the Dealership, at a windowed booth with a view of the diner's small, tree-lined, L-shaped parking lot. He was flipping through the pages of *Treasure Troves of Russian Art*, which he had found in the backseat of his car, and after his fourth cup of coffee, each caffeine-fueled flip threatened to tear the page from its spine.

He glanced at his Rolex, then out to the serene little parking lot, which seemed to calm him down for a few moments. He had to be patient, he told himself. Orlov's call would come. And he was sitting just a few feet away from the phone. Couldn't possibly miss it.

"So how will we know these two women?"

Benny and Carmine were parked in the last row at the top of the Empire Parking Garage. This was the tallest structure in Westchester County, with sweeping views of the Hudson River and its green, rolling valleys.

Benny turned off the engine. He looked at Carmine and shook his head. "Look around you, Carmine. Do you see anyone else up here?"

Carmine did a visual sweep of this top level auto aerie, and nodded. "Anyway, they'll look like Russian gangsters. Female gansters."

Bennie stared at his companion. "What—you mean like Natasha from Rocky and Bullwinkle?"

"Yeah! And what was her partner's name?"

"I don't know, I never watched that show."

Benny thought about this, but decided not to follow up with *then how did you know about Natasha?* What mob guy—or affiliate—would ever admit to watching cartoons when they were a kid. What mob guy would ever admit they were once a kid. "Wait," he said. "It's on the tip of my tongue…"

"Who gives a fuck? Listen, Carmine, I don't feel like rummaging through your brain droppings right now. I'm trying to make a plan."

"You…what? You don't have a plan yet?" Carmine's placid face quickly contorted into hyper vigilence. He did an eyeball scan of the shadowy surroundings, owl-like, only turning his neck.

"Hey! What are you afraid of all of a sudden? Women? Russians? Russian women? Ha!" Benny patted Carmine's arm. "Look, we're here to make a deal. And they want to deal too, or they never would have set up this meeting."

"Yeah, maybe." But Carmine was too tentative.

"We *need* this, Carmine! Don't you get it? It's our one chance to get out of this life alive."

"No one gets out of this life alive, Benny."

"Oh yeah? Benny Bianco does! Remember what I told you, Carmine. I'm a survivor. Stick with me."

Carmine sank lower into his seat. "I think they're here." Both men watched the white panel truck. It moved in a slow arc around the perimeter of the parking level, and came to a stop in the space behind them. "Is that them?" Carmine whispered.

"I can't see, I don't want to turn around."

"Just look in the mirror."

"I don't want them to see me looking in the mirror."

"Oh, for Chrissake!" Carmine growled. "I'll go—"

Carmine opened the passenger door halfway. The older Russian woman pulled it all the way open for him and motioned for him to get out. "Both of you," she said, bending slightly to see Benny with his hand on the ignition key.

"Looks like your friend was going to leave you here by yourself," said the woman.

Benny was out of the car and walking slowly to the passenger side. "Why would I do that?" he said with a nervous laugh.

"Because," said the younger woman, who stepped out from behind a column. "You are aware, I hope, that this is a very dangerous game you are playing."

"What's she talking about?" said Carmine, out of the corner of his mouth, keeping his eyes on the women.

"No, no. We're not playing a game, ladies."

Carmine winced. *Maybe don't call them ladies.*

"We're here to make a deal."

"Give us the egg. Then we will deal."

The men exchanged a look. Benny said, "We don't have the egg. It's still in the car you people sold to the Benigno mob."

The older woman smirked. "*You people?* What does this mean?"

"The Russians. The Odessa mob."

"You got that half-right," she replied. "We are Russians—"

"Yeah, anyone can tell by your accents," said Carmine.

Benny shot him a hard look. "But...you're not part of Odessa? A different faction, maybe?"

The younger woman was getting impatient with the cat and mouse game. She leaned in and whispered something to her comrade.

"It's getting late," said the older woman. "We must bring this to a close."

"Who...who are you?" said Benny.

"KGB. I'm afraid you are trying to make a pact with the wrong devil, gentlemen. We are shadowing the Russian mob in this country. Our job is to repatriate all the stolen art since the revolution, and return it to our people."

Benny was wide-eyed and silent. Carmine had never seen him at a loss for words, or more importantly, a plan B.

But Benny had one more trick up his sleeve. "That's perfect!" he exclaimed. "We know where a lot of it is! And we've worked with the FBI—"

The younger woman stepped behind her elder, who put her arm out protectively. "You work for the FBI?"

"No, no. We used to! And also for the LCN, the Italian mob."

"You are busy little men."

"Yeah," said Carmine. "So we could be really useful to you."

"I don't think so—"

"Sure," said Benny. "We could keep them off your tail. Give them some false leads."

"So...they are on our tail?"

Benny hesitated. If he said *no*, they would have no reason to worry, and no need for their help. If he said *yes*, they might panic and flee, leaving him and Carmine back at square one, up to their own devices. Which, so far, had not served them very well. On the other hand, they might enlist their services to help them evade the Feds.

He needed the right answer. "Yes."

Apparently, that was not it. On a silent signal between the two, the younger woman pulled a small syringe from her coat pocket. She stuck the tip into a vial and drew in enough fluid to fill it. She took a step towards Benny.

"What the hell are you doing?" Benny backed away slowly, and both woman advanced at a leisurely pace, until they had him corraled against the garage wall. He tried to duck under, then around them, keeping his arms wrapped around his neck. He was sure they would go for his neck. They had some sort of anesthetic in that vial and they would knock out both of them, maybe take them prisoner, use them to bargain their way out of the arms of US law enforcement.

That was what Benny was thinking, when both women forced him against the wall and then, before he could understand what was happening, they lifted him up with arms under his knees, and tipped him over the ledge. Benny plunged to the street from the tallest structure in the city of Yonkers, and no one even watched him on the way down.

Carmine backed up toward the center of the garage and looked around frantically for help. But there was no one coming, or going.

The women conferred for a moment, then approached, their mouths set in grim determination. "What do they say in that beer commercial?" said the older woman.

The younger woman brandished the syringe at Benny. "This one's for you."

So he was going to die. This is how Carmine Rizzo would meet the death he had been expecting for so much of his life. But not at the hands of Victor Benigno or Dante Forte. Not even in a shoot-out with the FBI. He would be killed, in real life, by cartoonish KGB villains. His next thought was Lorena, but before he could form his last mental picture of his wife— there she was, in the flesh, in her brother-in-law's car, emerging from the ramp as if shot out of a cannon. She roared toward where he stood facing the women, horn blaring, bright lights piercing the gloom. He thought he was dreaming, but yes, it was Lorena, all right.

He could make out her head now, hair pulled close with a hairnet, her face dusted with flour—just generally looking as if she had made a snap decision to find him. Her man. Carmine.

She pulled to within inches of the women, threatening to mow them down. The younger one shook the syringe at the car and its occupant, but it was no match for a two-ton vehicle. "Carmy!" Lorena screamed. "Get the fuck in!"

The women walked toward the driver side, and Lorena pressed the lock. They went around the rear of the car to the passenger side just as Carmine pulled the door closed. The window was down, and the younger woman stabbed at Carmine's neck with the syringe.

"You bitch!" Lorena screamed, and when she pressed the pedal to the floor the car took off like a shot, and screeched along the perimeter of the lot, as Lorena looked for the exit. She was disoriented in the confusion— back was front, left was right—and she had to circle around twice, pinning the KGB agents against the wall as they tried to avoid being mowed down by this flour-dappled, hairnet wearing lunatic.

Carmine, meanwhile, grasped the edges of his seat as he gazed in awe at Lorena—wife, baker, savior.

"Hold on!" Lorena took a sharp left turn down the ramp, scraping the mirror on the concrete wall. Down, down they spiraled through the parking garage— oblivious to the phalanx of official US government vehicles climbing up in the opposite corner.

Sirens blaring, lights flashing, they reached the top level just in time to see the Russian agents drive towards the exit. One FBI vehicle blocked the ramp, while the rest surrounded the departing women.

"Get out of the car. Hands in the air," called an Officer through his bullhorn.

There was a tense moment. The women conferred silently, and then they both emerged, hands in the air, pushing the doors open with their legs. Two officers approached, and one held back, as he spoke into his collar. "We're here. We have them."

"Stay with them, we're on our way," said Mark Oberlin.

The police trained their guns on the women, who were backing up almost imperceptibly. "Don't move!" he shouted, and suddenly all eyes were on the ramp, as the FBI surveillance van appeared, with Mark Oberlin and crew inside.

Someone yelled, "Stop them!"

The women were running towards the edge of the building, the older one in front.

"Hold your fire!" said Oberlin, grabbing the bullhorn from the uniformed officer.

The women pressed their backs to the wall, the older, taller one craned her neck to see over the edge, and Oberlin thought she might jump.

"Don't!" he called out.

But then she looked back and smiled as the helicopter that had been hovering high above the landscape, above the fray at Dan's Driveaway

Dealership, suddenly swooped low over the building. A sling descended from the helicopter. The older woman grabbed it, slipped it on and motioned at the pilot to pull up.

"Nyet!" The younger woman made a grab for her companion's foot.

"Don't be stupid! We will send another one for you!"

For a moment, the helicopter and the KGB agent hovered over the parking garage.

Oberlin called out, "Let them go!" He'd never hear the end of it if his actions caused the helicopter to crash into the street below.

The younger agent made another attempt to grab the leg of her comrade. But her comrade pulled away, and she fell, silently, to the street, where she came to rest a few feet away from the body of Benny Cataldo.

In a quiet neighborhood on the outskirts of town, Nick and Debbie, test driving the BMW, picked up a couple of friends with open beer cans. "Careful with that," said Nick.

"Being careful," said one friend, lowering the window and tossing the can onto the street.

"Don't do that," said Nick, slamming on the brakes. "Go on. Pick it up."

The friend opened the back door and went to recover the can. The other friend picked up the Faberge egg that had slid into the back of the car from under the front seat. He held it up to the rear view mirror. "Hey! Look what I found!"

Debbie turned around. "Hey, that's really pretty. Looks like an egg."

Everyone was back in the car and Nick started off. The first friend rolled down his window, grabbed the egg, and took aim at the street.

"Don't!" cried Debbie.

"Just kidding."

"Someone obviously forgot it in the car. They might contact the dealer to get it back."

"It's a piece of junk. Plastic rhinestones and gold paint—"

"Just give it to me!" Debbie reached back and grabbed the egg. "It may be junk to everyone else, but it could be precious to the person who misplaced it."

"Hey," said Nick, "I really gotta get this baby back to the dealership."

He stopped at the end of the street and they piled boisterously out of the car, with two cans of beer hanging from the remains of the plastic casing. "Be careful," he warned. "No drinking and walking!"

The friends gave a synchronized finger-salute to the departing BMW, and cracked open the beer cans.

"You know something," said Nick to Debbie. "It's pretty crazy that these dealerships trust people off the street with their cars."

"Well, luckily for them, you're very responsible," Debbie replied, patting his arm.

"Do you think *they* think we're really interested in buying this?"

Debbie shrugged. "The salesman has to take a chance, I guess. When we return it I'm sure someone else will want to try it out."

"Test drive. It's called a test drive."

"Yeah. Whatever."

Nick turned onto the highway, four blocks away from the dealership.

"Wow, look at all those flashing lights. Wonder what happened…"

"Accident, probably. Hope they didn't close the street."

But they did close the street, about two blocks away from the dealership. Nick put on his turn signal and pulled onto a side street. "Better go in the side entrance." But the side entrance to the dealership was cordoned off with police tape. Two cruisers were parked in front, blocking the entrance.

Nick lowered his window and called out to one of the cops. "Hey, this is a demo. I need to return it."

The cop looked at him for a tense moment, then shook his head. "You can't go in. There's an active investigation."

Nick's face went red -hot. "Hey, look. The salesman didn't say exactly when I needed to get this back…"

"Yeah," called Debbie, ducking her head to see out of Nick's window. "We've really only had it out for twenty minutes…"

The cop approached the car, hand on his pistol hip. His partner hoisted his 6'5" frame out of the patrol car and stood beside it, making it look like a toy.

"What are you talking about?" said the approaching officer.

"We didn't steal this car, officer!" said Nick, slightly frantic. "It's a demo!"

The officer exchanged a glance with his giant partner, then looked at Nick with a wide grin. "That's very funny…"

"Is it?"

"Yeah. Look, we're conducting an investigation, nothing to do with your demo car. This is an active crime scene, and it's closed to the public."

"But…what do we do with the car?" called Debbie from over Nick's right shoulder. "We need to return it."

The cop shrugged, because this was not his problem. But he was not without sympathy. "I dunno. I'd probably just park it across the street at the diner for now, and leave a note and the keys with the people over there."

Nick nodded, relieved that the decision had been made for him. "And they can contact the dealership manager. Is that it?"

"Yeah, sure." The cop was about to leave, but then he leaned into the window of the car, coming nose to nose with Nick. "You're a real oddball, you know that?"

"What…why?"

"You never even asked what's going on here, with all the police activity. I dunno. I just find that strange."

"Ha, yeah. I guess I was so wrapped up in my own thoughts…"

"You do that a lot," Debbie added.

"So, what *did* happen?" Nick said, "Grand theft auto?" He looked from the cop to Debbie to see if his minor quip had hit home.

But Debbie stared at him open-mouthed, and the cop gave him a long, hard look. "I can't release any information to the public at this time." With that he straightened up, backed away from the BMW, and walked—with long important strides—back to his patrol car.

"That was weird." Nick put the car in gear, drove around the corner to the diner, and pulled into the lot.

Back at the diner, Dante Forte sits stoically, awaiting the promised *"game on"* call from the late Peter Orlov. He is dimly aware of the muted sounds of police activity, sirens and horns, that bleed through the plate glass windows, but it's the sudden, steady whir of helicopter blades—an intolerable assault to his senses—that he cannot ignore. He stands up, pulls a coin from his pocket and drops it into the jukebox at his booth. He flips through the titles and, failing to locate Vivaldi, settles on the Bee Gee's *Tragedy.*

Nick pulls into the parking lot of the diner and parks the BMW near the entrance, in full view of Dante's booth. "What are you doing with that?" says Nick, when Debbie pulls the egg from the car and tucks it into her tote.

"Taking it home! I'll call the dealership tomorrow, or whenever the place is open again."

"I hope there's someone in charge who can take the keys," says Nick.

"Don't worry. Just find the manager and explain. We don't want them to think we stole a BMW."

"Okay, and maybe you should call a taxi."

So the young couple enter the diner and everything goes according to plan. The manager is a sympathetic woman who gets into an animated conversation with Nick about what might have happened at the dealership to create such a commotion.

In the diner's little vestibule, Debbie sets her tote on the floor, drops a coin into the payphone and calls the local taxi service.

Dante has decided he's waited long enough. He leaves his booth and walks a few feet to the inner door of the vestibule and hears someone else using the phone. He cracks the door to let them know he is waiting, and the door pushes Debbie's tote to the floor, spilling all its contents.

"Oh, so sorry," says Dante, trying to push open the door. But Debbie's behind is holding it shut as she bends to repatriate her belongings.

"Back off!" she calls. She opens the door and squeezes past Dante, giving him a side-eye. The top of the egg is visible in the tote, among her hastily retrieved possessions.

Dante takes the phone, wipes off the mouthpiece with his handkerchief, and drops a coin in the slot. "Dan's Driveaway Dealership," he says to Information. He's connected to the main office, and the call goes straight to the answering machine. "Peter Orlov, this is…" he begins, then has second thoughts about leaving his name on the tape. "This is a courtesy call from the Diner. Your pick-up order is ready." He hangs up. It's time to get back to business, and business is always more productive in person. *And the little rat has my hundred grand… Okay, Victor's hundred grand.*

"Thanks again!" Nick calls back to the manager as he and Debbie leave the diner. They encounter Dante, wide-eyed, mouth agape, as he surveys the scene at Dan's Driveaway Dealership. "Really something, right?" says Nick. "We tried to return our demo, but the whole place is roped off. Cops all over the place."

"Wha…what happened?"

"They closed the lot. Couldn't return the car, so—"

"He means, what happened at the dealership," said Debbie, still giving Dante the evil eye for dumping her stuff.

"Oh, yeah. Cops wouldn't tell us anything, but it's crazy activity, right? Even the helicopter—you don't see that every day."

Dante was only half-listening, his eyes now drawn to the bejewelled egg sitting on top of Debbie's tote bag. He pointed to it. "Is that—"

But before he was able to fully articulate his query—*Is that my fucking Faberge egg?*—a white police van, lights and sirens at full power, came to a stop a few feet away, and addressed him with the disembodied voice of Mark Oberlin. "Dante Forte, put your hands on your head and approach the van slowly."

Dante did as he was told, and ducked into the waiting van after a parting, puzzled glance at the young couple with the egg. *His egg. Well, okay. Victor's egg.*

Inside the police van, Dante found himself face to face with Mark Oberlin, and three other agents. He felt a tap on his shoulder and turned around, coming nose to nose with Sandra B. "What are you doing here?"

"No talking," said Oberlin. "You're both material witnesses."

"Why doesn't he get Mirandered?" Sandra demanded. "That's the first thing you did when you pulled me into this shitty van."

"It's *Miranda*," said Dante. "In which case you should say *Miranda-ed.*"

"Oh go blow your nose, Mr. Egghead. If you were so smart you wouldn't have spent the past two hours in a diner with the world coming apart right in front of you—"

"No talking," Oberlin tried again.

"It was happening behind me!" said Dante. "I was facing the other way!"

Oberlin rolled his eyes. *Here it comes.*

"Ha! How lame can you get! I take it back—"

"Take *what* back?"

"You can't possibly be Billy's father. You're too dumb. I don't know what I ever saw in you—"

"Must have been something, Sandra. Back then I couldn't peel you off me!"

"People!" Oberlin shouted so loudly that the driver pulled to a stop at the side of the road. "There seems to be a difference of opinion on the nature and quality of your past relationship."

"No shit!" said Sandra.

"Well, here's a simple solution. Since Victor knew you both back then, why don't you open up the discussion to include his thoughts on the subject."

Sandra and Dante unlocked eyeballs and sat back in their seats. Not another word was spoken for the rest of the ride.

28

The New York FBI office was buzzing with activity. The failed Auto/ ArtTheft sting, which led to no arrests, had unwittingly uncovered espionage activity by the KGB on U.S. soil, and Ken Schneider—who claimed all the credit by virtue of the fact that as SAC, he *could*— was now a hero. He put D'Angelo in charge of the new Russian Organized Crime squad—ROC—owing to the fact that Mark Oberlin had a habit of losing or misplacing his informants.

Mark Oberlin pondered his losses. Benny was dead, his body lying next to a woman later dentified as a Russian operative. She might have been Benny's killer—or it might have been the KGB agent who flew off in the helicopter, which seemed to have disappeared from the skies and was probably sitting on some oligarch's helipad in the Hamptons. Schneider's new ROC squad leader, D'Angelo, would find her. Or not.

And what about Peter Orlov? Poor Peter. Just trying to help out, and ended up taking a needle for the team. Collateral damage from a sting gone wrong. Maybe the victims, the witnesses *and* the perpetrators were one and the same. And all were dead.

Except for Carmine Rizzo.

"Where is Carmine?" Schneider had asked, as the bodies were being packed up. "Oberlin, have you lost your TEI again?"

But Carmine wasn't lost. He was sitting beside Lorena—in her brother's wife's cousin's car—driving down to Florida.

He was pretty sure no one would look for them at Disney World. Besides, it was well past time for a second honeymoon with his lovely wife.

"No amount of Law enforcement can solve a problem that goes back to the family."
—*J. Edgar Hoover*

Printed in the United States
by Baker & Taylor Publisher Services